The Healing of Texas Jake

The Cat Pack

Books by Phyllis Reynolds Naylor

Witch's Sister
Witch Water
The Witch Herself
Walking Through the Dark
How I Came to Be a Writer
How Lazy Can You Get?
Eddie, Incorporated
All Because I'm Older
Shadows on the Wall
Faces in the Water
Footprints at the Window
The Boy with the Helium Head
A String of Chances
The Solomon System
Bernie Magruder and the Case of the Big Stink
Night Cry
Old Sadie and the Christmas Bear
The Dark of the Tunnel
The Agony of Alice
The Keeper
Bernie Magruder and the Disappearing Bodies
The Year of the Gopher
Beetles, Lightly Toasted
Maudie in the Middle
One of the Third Grade Thonkers
Alice in Rapture, Sort Of
Keeping a Christmas Secret
Bernie Magruder and the Haunted Hotel
Send No Blessings
Reluctantly Alice
King of the Playground
Shiloh
All but Alice
Josie's Troubles
The Grand Escape
Alice in April
Bernie Magruder and the Drive-Thru Funeral Parlor

Alice In-Between
The Fear Place
Alice the Brave
Being Danny's Dog
Ice
Bernie Magruder and the Bus Station Blowup
Alice in Lace
Shiloh Season
Ducks Disappearing
Outrageously Alice
The Healing of Texas Jake
I Can't Take You Anywhere
Saving Shiloh
Bernie Magruder and the Pirate's Treasure
Achingly Alice
Danny's Desert Rats
Sang Spell
Sweet Strawberries
Alice on the Outside
Walker's Crossing
Jade Green
Bernie Magruder and the Parachute Peril
The Grooming of Alice
Carlotta's Kittens
Alice Alone
Please Do Feed the Bears
Simply Alice
Blizzard's Wake
Starting with Alice
Bernie Magruder and the Bats in the Belfry
Patiently Alice
Alice in Blunderland
Including Alice
Lovingly Alice
Polo's Mother

The Healing of Texas Jake

The Cat Pack

By Phyllis Reynolds Naylor

Illustrated by Alan Daniel

Aladdin Paperbacks

New York London Toronto Sydney

To Adam, Benjamin, and Nathaniel Lanman

ALADDIN PAPERBACKS
An imprint of Simon & Schuster Children's Publishing Division
1230 Avenue of the Americas, New York, NY 10020
Text copyright © 1997 by Phyllis Reynolds Naylor
Illustrations copyright © 1997 by Alan Daniel
All rights reserved, including the right of reproduction
in whole or in part in any form.
ALADDIN PAPERBACKS and colophon are registered
trademarks of Simon & Schuster, Inc.
Also available in an Atheneum Books for Young Readers hardcover edition.
The text of this book was set in Goudy Old Style.
Manufactured in the United States of America
This Aladdin Paperbacks edition May 2005
2 4 6 8 10 9 7 5 3 1
The Library of Congress has cataloged the hardcover edition as follows:
Naylor, Phyllis Reynolds.
The healing of Texas Jake/by Phyllis Reynolds Naylor ;
illustrated by Alan Daniel—1st ed.
Sequel to: The grand escape.
Summary: To prove themselves worthy of succeeding Texas Jake as leader of the feline
Club of Mysteries, cat brothers Marco and Polo agree to bring him to the comfrey
that will heal his wounds.
ISBN 0-689-81124-1 (hc.)
[1. Cats—Fiction.] I. Daniel, Alan, ill. II. Title.
PZ7.N24He 1997
[Fic]—dc20
96-22025
ISBN 0-689-87406-5 (pbk.)

CONTENTS

1
WAITING FOR T. J.

When the broad, dry leaves of the sycamore made scratching sounds against the windowpane, and the wild October wind raced recklessly down the alley, Polo worried.

For a week now his brother Marco, the second silver tabby, had been strutting back and forth in front of the mirror up in the Neals' bedroom. Every day he had murmured to his reflection, "You magnificent cat, you!" and, "What a splendid creature you are!"

It could only mean one thing: Marco was preparing to return to the Club of Mysteries, this time, perhaps, as its new leader.

No one had seen Texas Jake since he'd bravely defended the club against Bertram the Bad, the huge mastiff who lived a few blocks away. No one knew just how serious his injuries were. But word had traveled from alley to alley, house to house, cat to cat that when the leaves were falling and the moon was full, T. J. would be back. Whether or not he would be strong enough to be their commander again, Lord of the Loft, King of the Alley, Cat Supreme, nobody knew. But because the leaves were falling and the moon was full, Marco announced to his brother that it was time to go.

Marco and Polo were as good as gold all day so that the Neals would let them out. They cleaned each other's ears. They shared their catnip with Jumper and Spinner, the kittens the Neals had adopted the last time the tabbies had gone off, fearing they would never see Marco and Polo again. Marco and Polo even took their hairball medicine without a fuss, and restrained themselves when they heard the sound of a can opener about six o'clock, as Mrs. Neal did not like cats brushing against her legs when she was making dinner.

It wasn't until the Neals sat down to enjoy their own meal that Marco and Polo went to the back door and meowed.

At last Mrs. Neal put down her fork. "Oh, Roger, I wish you had never left the side door open last month so those cats could get out. Now that Marco and Polo have been out in the world, they'll never be happy as house cats again. I've seen them hanging around with that motley crew in Murphy's garage, and who knows what they're doing."

"What's done is done," said her husband. "We'll just have to trust them and hope for the best."

And while Jumper and Spinner watched enviously from

the window, on the doorstep Marco and Polo gave their paws a final lick, tidied their tails, and set off.

If the contest were between him and Marco as to which of them would become Texas Jake's replacement, Polo decided, it would have to be Marco, no question about it, because Marco could read. All these years they had been using the same litter box, Marco sat there studying the newspapers on the bottom, learning to spell, while Polo simply did his business and climbed out.

But there were other members of the club to be considered as well. How did Boots feel about a new leader and who did Elvis see as Commander in Chief? For all Polo knew, even Carlotta might like a turn at being Number One.

It was cold in the alley on this late October night. Outside smelled different from inside; the inside of the Neals' house smelled of pot roast and potatoes, of perfume and soap, of coffee, books, and blankets. But outside smelled of moldy leaves, garbage cans, damp dank earth, and, worst of all, dog.

Here the grass was dry, the leaves crisp, the air cool, and the wind sharp against their ears and noses. There were scurryings, scuttlings, scratchings, rustlings, squealings, screechings, squawkings, and honkings, so that Marco's and Polo's ears were moving constantly, their whiskers twitching, paws pausing now and then as they walked single file down the narrow alley and up the steps in the dusty darkness to the loft in Murphy's garage.

It was as black as a cat's nose in the loft. Still, Polo

could just make out the familiar shape of the old rocking chair where Texas used to sit. The army cot. The bookcase, the lamp, and the bird cage.

To tell the truth, Polo preferred inside to outside. If he could live whatever kind of life he liked, he would leave the warm, comfortable home of the Neals just long enough to have a quick adventure, and be back in time for breakfast.

When he and Marco went out together, however, they might be gone for days—a week, even—with no meals served in a porcelain bowl, no velveteen basket in which to sleep, no water except what they might find in the rim of a garbage can lid from a recent rain.

But the thought of Marco going somewhere without him—especially going somewhere with the calico cat named Carlotta—was unbearable. So wherever his brother went, Polo went, too. But he always glanced longingly over his shoulder at the Neals' back door and hoped he wasn't seeing it for the very last time.

"There's no one here," he whispered to Marco in the quiet of the loft. "Are you sure this is the right night?"

"There hasn't been a fuller moon than this," said Marco. "If not tonight, then when?"

The stairs creaked softly behind them and the tabbies turned to see two green eyes. The eyes seemed to be floating in space because they were surrounded by darkness. But gradually Polo could tell that the eyes belonged to a very black cat. And when the very black cat opened its mouth and gave a very loud yowl that started low and traveled

5

high, wavered up and down like a roller coaster, and finally dissolved in a growl, Polo knew it was Elvis.

"It's only us," Marco said. "Marco and Polo."

"How *is* everyone?" asked Polo, hoping for news of Carlotta.

"Boots is as ornery as ever," Elvis told him. "Got in a fight last week with one of the Over-the-Hill Gang, but he came out with hardly a scratch. I, of course, am busy with my concerts and had an audience of two dozen the night before last. I never sang better, if I do say so myself."

"And Carlotta?" Polo asked.

"Ah! Carlotta!" Elvis sighed. "Can't say I've seen her lately. She used to attend all my concerts, but—like most she-cats—Carlotta's fickle."

Marco and Polo grew quiet. It was always a worry when a cat hadn't been seen for some time. At that moment, however, there were more soft creakings on the stairs, and Polo stared through the darkness hoping to see the delicate form of the calico cat who had captured his heart and Marco's as well.

It was Boots, a small white cat with brown on the ends of his paws.

"Am I late?" he asked, sniffing each cat in turn to make sure he was a bona fide member and not a spy from the Over-the-Hill Gang.

"No, you're early," Elvis told him. "We're still waiting for T. J."

"And Carlotta," Polo added. "Has anyone seen her?"

"I did, a few days ago at the Fishmonger," said Boots.

6

"It's a new restaurant at the other end of the alley. They didn't lock their leftovers away in a Dumpster the way the Big Burger did. We're back to big metal garbage cans and the most amazing array of delicacies you can't find anywhere else."

Elvis agreed. "Fillet of cod, rainbow trout, fried perch . . . the Fishmonger is the answer to a cat's prayers."

"Indeed, I noticed an ad for them in the newspaper," said Marco. "They specialize in crab cakes, I believe."

It did sound wonderful, but Polo wanted to see Carlotta more than he wanted to try out the Fishmonger. He wanted to see Carlotta even more than he wished to be back at the Neals'. Just to have her brush up against him, rub his nose, and tweak his whiskers would be enough.

"Maybe Texas isn't coming. He was always the first one here before," said Marco finally, wondering if he should hop up on the old rocker where Texas always sat, and declare himself king before any of the other cats tried it.

"The moon is full," said Boots.

"And the leaves have begun to fall," said Elvis. "That's when we agreed to meet."

"But has anyone *seen* him? Actually *seen* him?" asked Polo.

"I heard he was getting better," said Boots.

"I heard he was taking a little food," said Elvis.

"I heard he has been lounging about on his master's porch," said Boots. "But no, I haven't actually *seen* him."

"Nor I," said Marco.

"Nor I," said Polo.

7

Marco stood, stretched, and took a few steps toward the rocker. He noticed that Elvis had also moved a few steps closer on the other side.

"If the unthinkable has happened . . . ," Marco began.

"And our leader has passed away . . . ," continued Elvis.

"Then we need a new one," Boots said. "And I want you all to know that I am prepared . . ."

"I would be most happy to . . . ," said Elvis.

"I am ready to become your new Commander in Chief, Lord of the Loft, King of the Alley, Feline Leader, and Cat Supreme!" said Marco, his voice even louder than before.

At this, Boots also edged closer to the rocking chair, the throne. Slowly the cats began to circle in the darkness, low growls coming from their throats, and all Polo could see were their yellow and green eyes, and an occasional flash of a whisker in the moonlight.

"Perhaps if Texas Jake doesn't come, there could be an election!" Polo said plaintively as the growls turned into yowls and hisses.

Suddenly, from out of the darkness, a deep voice boomed: "HE HAS COME!"

Polo jumped six inches off the floor and spun around, bumping into Boots, who was doing the same. With fur rising, backs arched, tails thickened, and ears pressed flat against their heads, the cats strained to see where the voice was coming from.

And then, from an old hassock at the very back of the loft, where he had been sitting all this time, a large yellow cat with a white belly slowly made his way down onto the floor and came limping stiffly over to the others.

Even though he was hurt, even though he was lame, even though he had seventeen stitches in his side, four in one of his paws, and two in his nose, Texas Jake walked with his head high. And when he got to the little circle of cats waiting for him in the middle of the floor, his cold yellow eyes fell on each one in turn, before they settled at last on Marco.

9

2
WHAT CATS ARE FOR

Instantly the cats froze in their tracks. Polo hardly dared to breathe. Texas Jake limped over to the old rocker and struggled to hop up on it. His yellow eyes were his most visible feature—them and his white belly. Gradually he settled back to observe the cats below.

"So!" he said, and just the way he said it made their hair stand on end. "Old T. J.'s on the sick list and already they're makin' his coffin, are they?"

"Oh, no, Texas!" Boots said. "We just thought . . ."

"Just thought you'd be lookin' for my replacement, eh? A new Lord of the Loft, King of the Alley, Cat Supreme?" And T. J.'s yellow eyes grew narrower still as he studied Marco.

The full moon came out from behind a cloud just then and the loft was filled with the dusky white of moon glow. Marco and Polo, along with Boots and Elvis, crouched sullenly on the floor beneath the stern gaze of Texas Jake.

"We were only discussing 'what ifs,' Texas," said Boots.

"We wanted the Club of Mysteries to go on, and without you as our leader we wondered what we would do," Marco added.

"I see! So you, who have only been a member a couple of weeks, are already making big-shot talk, commander talk, take-charge-when-old-Texas-kicks-the-bucket talk," said Texas, his voice ending in a deep growl.

"All I meant," said Marco, "was that *if* anything happened to you, I would be deeply honored to serve the Club of Mysteries half as well as you have done, Texas."

That may have made Texas Jake a bit happier, Polo wasn't sure, but it didn't do anything to soothe the other cats.

"*You* would be deeply honored?" Elvis hissed. "Why, you're not even dry behind the ears yet. What *you* know about our club is hardly worth the whiskers on a mouse."

"Oh, but Marco can reeead," Texas Jake said, drawing out the word. "And a cat who can *reeead* thinks he is better than all the other cats in the world."

"He can read, but can he sing?" asked Elvis. "Has he ever composed a song in his life? If I had to choose between a cat who could read and a cat who could sing, I'd take music any day."

Polo was conscious of a low hissing sound filling the loft, and discovered that Boots's tail was growing thick, his ears laid back. "You are both wrong," Boots meowed, his green eyes darting from Elvis to Marco and back again.

"What is reading and what is singing if a cat does not have his wits about him? A leader of cats needs to be clever above everything else, and I, I dare say, am that cat."

"*You?*" cried Elvis. "Why, you are the smallest cat here, a mere shrimp of a cat!"

And suddenly the cats were circling again, spitting and hissing, low growls coming from their throats. The yowling became louder and louder as their backs rose and arched once more.

"*Stop* it!" came a voice from the stairs, and suddenly a calico cat trotted daintily across the floor of the loft, her tail held high in the air.

"Carlotta!" cried all the he-cats together. And at once a great nose rubbing, whisker tweaking, ear licking, and deep-chested purring began in the loft.

"I've missed you all!" said Carlotta. "Each and every one of you. So what is all this quarreling about?" And she stood up on her hind legs, resting her front paws on the rocker, to give Texas a little lick on the nose.

"Well, it seems the lads have so much kindness in their hearts, they were arguing over who would replace me after I'm gone," said Texas.

"What?" cried Carlotta.

"Why do we need a leader at all?" asked Polo. "Why can't we just be equal friends?"

Texas Jake was so startled he almost fell off the rocker. "Equal friends?" he cried. "No leader? Without a leader, my lad, this club would go straight to the dogs."

Carlotta agreed. "Polo," she purred, "can you imagine a car without a driver? A chicken without a head?"

"There must be one cat above all others who can lead a discussion, for without a leader we would find ourselves talking about anything except life's mysteries," Texas explained. "Without a leader we might even find ourselves pondering how many mice could dance on the head of a pin."

"How many mice *could* dance on the head of a pin?" asked Boots, who was confused.

"That's just it!" cried Texas. "It's a stupid question. Are we talking about big mice or little mice? Live or dead? A straight pin or a bowling pin? That, my lads, is the kind of talk you get without a leader."

The cats grew very quiet in the presence of such wisdom. As the cold wind blew through the back window of the loft and seeped in around the cracks, Carlotta snuggled against Boots, who had curled up beside Elvis, who was lying, in turn, next to Marco and Polo.

"And with you as our leader, Texas, what great mystery should we be discussing instead?" asked Carlotta.

"Perhaps the greatest mystery of all," Texas told her, settling back down and preparing to enjoy himself. "What is the meaning of life? Why were cats put on this earth in the first place?"

Polo thought about that one. What *was* the meaning of life, and of what use were he and Marco?

"To eat and sleep and lie in the sun?" he asked.

"No, no, no!" said Texas. "Pigs eat and sleep and lie in the sun! Dogs do the same. Even snakes lie in the sun! Have we no nobler mission than that?"

"To sing and make music in a troubled world?" suggested Elvis.

"Even more noble than that," said Texas Jake. "More noble, even, than reeeading!" When it appeared that none of the cats could guess the reason cats were put on the earth, Texas answered for them: "To teach our masters patience, lads! Think about it. Do you remember when we were only kittens and our masters were introducing us to the litter box? What were we teaching our masters then?"

"Patience," replied all the cats together.

"And when we meowed to get out the front door, then walked around and meowed to get in the back, what were we teaching our masters?"

"Patience," replied all the cats again.

"And when our masters start down the stairs in the morning and we walk just ahead of them, in the very spot they want to put their feet, what are we teaching them? Let's hear it loud and clear!"

"Patience!" all the cats cried together.

"There is no nobler purpose in life than to teach the two-leggeds patience," said Texas. "That is our purpose and that is our goal. It's questions like these that we discuss in the Club of Mysteries, and the reason that there must always be a leader, a Cat Supreme."

Even as he said it, however, he seemed tired. Just the act of thinking so hard seemed to take all his strength, and the big yellow cat stretched out his front paws, rested his head upon them, and closed his yellow eyes.

All the other cats did the same, but Marco was thinking. Somehow this had not seemed like a discussion at all. Texas asked the questions and answered them himself. And before Marco could stop himself, he heard a low growl coming from his throat.

Not a head raised, but every cat in the loft opened one eye.

"Excuse me," said Marco hurriedly. "My stomach." But it was a long, long time before he fell asleep.

3
DINNER MUSIC

It was Carlotta who suggested they go to the Fishmonger for dinner to celebrate their being together again.

"There is nothing like a little fish in the belly to bring out the best in a feline," she purred.

Polo was hopelessly in love with the beautiful calico, but so was every other cat in the loft, and he knew that he would have to be content with a lick here, a nose rub there, and a snuggle once in a while when she was feeling sleepy.

All the cats roused themselves and stretched, and after Texas Jake managed to drag his injured body off the rocking chair and down the stairs, they set off up the alley.

By now they all realized that when they'd gathered there in the loft, Texas had been waiting for them, just out of sight. They knew he had heard every word they had said, and Marco was only glad he had not said more.

The restaurant was a long, low building with lots of windows in the front and back. Through the glass Marco could see candles atop each table, families enjoying their dinners. Wafting through the air was a delicious smell, even better than the smells at Big Burger. Never mind that Mrs. Neal had fed the cats before she let them out. A cat's philosophy is: When food is available, eat it; one never knows when a mouse might cross one's path again.

"Ah!" said Marco, reading a sign in the window. "Weekly specials: Monday: seafood buffet; Tuesday: fish fry, all you can eat . . ." He was going to read the menu for the rest of the week when he realized that as far as Texas was concerned, he was simply showing off, so he shut up. All the cats grew quiet, waiting for Texas's permission to eat.

"Now we have to be careful," Texas warned, still glaring at Marco. "We don't want to be chased away as we were at the Big Burger. No knocking over the trash cans, lads. No rattling of lids, if you please."

With a graceful leap, Carlotta bounded to the rim of one garbage can, its lid askew, and disappeared inside, with only the tip of her tail showing. The other cats followed, each to a different can, and soon the air was filled with hungry slurps and happy purrings.

It was difficult, however, for Texas Jake to balance on the rim of a garbage can, Marco noticed. And since he fully intended to become Commander in Chief himself, Lord of the Alley, Cat Supreme, he decided he could afford to be kind to the big tomcat.

Turning to Texas, he said, "If you would allow me, T. J.,

just tell me what you would like for dinner and I'll get it for you."

The yellow cat turned his head slowly and his great yellow eyes studied Marco. Was that a smile on his face, Marco wondered, or a sneer?

"Whatever I want, lad? What I want is a whole salmon. Not a chunk, not a head, not a fin or a tail, but a whole fish. A salmon."

Marco swallowed.

"That would be almost as big as you are, Texas!" Carlotta said, peeping over the rim of a garbage can.

"He asked what I wanted, my dear, and that's what I want," Texas told her. "Now I shall sit over there by the wall and wait for my friend Marco to bring me dinner." And with that, Texas lumbered stiffly to the back of the parking lot.

What had he gotten himself into? Marco wondered. He had never seen a whole salmon, either dead or alive. As he remembered from the tidbits Mrs. Neal sometimes put in his porcelain dish, it had a red or pinkish color, but would he know one if he saw it? Nonetheless, he hopped up on a garbage can, took a deep breath, leaned toward the sweet fish-smelling goo, and dived in.

Elvis was the first cat to finish, and when Texas Jake saw him taking his place at the far end of the wall, getting ready for a concert, he said, "By all means, let there be music! But make it something light. What these old bones of mine need now is laughter and song."

The sleek black cat licked the fried flounder off his paws and then, raising his head so that he could see out over the parking lot, he said, "I composed a little ditty just yesterday, Texas, that I think you might enjoy.

> Sing a song of frog legs
> And fish for Texas Jake,
> Four and twenty frog legs,
> Baked in a cake.
> When the cake was frosted,
> The frogs began to jump,
> Turned it into such a mess
> We tossed it in the dump.

The cats all meowed their approval of Elvis's new song. But there were other cats waiting their chance to perform—a Persian with a huge fluffy tail, a Siamese with blue eyes, and an Abyssinian with a mournful face.

The Persian took his place next, beside Elvis, and did his number. From deep inside the garbage can, where he was still hunting for salmon, Marco heard him sing:

> This lot is your lot,
> This lot is my lot,
> From Murphy's alley,
> Down to the corner,
> From the picket fences,
> To tin-roof tool sheds.
> This lot was made for you and me.

The cats all meowed again, and urged the Siamese with the blue eyes to go next, even though his voice was more

like a whine than a meow. The Siamese was also tempera-
mental, and hissed softly at Elvis and the Persian to get out
of the way so he could have the stage to himself. And he
would not sing until he had the full attention of every cat
in the parking lot.

When every cat was listening at last, the Siamese
opened his mouth and wailed:

> Oh, bury me not
> On the lone prairie
> Where prairie dogs
> Will walk o'er me.
> Where rats and mice
> Will roam so free,
> Oh, bury me not
> On the lone prairie.

Texas Jake began to bristle, and the other members of
the Club of Mysteries could see that he did not like songs
about cats dying and being buried. Texas commanded
respect in the alley, and as soon as the Siamese realized his
mistake, he stopped singing at once and slunk back off the
wall.

The Abyssinian was the last cat to perform. His hair
hung low about his face and his eyes looked sad. With great
gravity he took his place at the end of the wall, wiped his
whiskers, and began:

> Does your tail hang low?
> Does it wobble to and fro?

Can you tie it in a knot?
Can you tie it in a bow?
Can you sling it over your shoulder
Like a Continental soldier?
Does your tail . . . hang . . . low?

Marco, who had no luck in the first garbage can and was trying a second, thought that was about the stupidest song he had ever heard, especially the way the Abyssinian sang it. But Elvis had joined the Abyssinian now, along with the Siamese and Persian for the traditional cat quartet. Marco looked out to see the four cats leaning their heads together:

Shine on, shine on harvest moon
Up in the sky.
I . . . ain't . . . had no salmon since
January, February, June or July . . .

Suddenly the cats felt the hair on their necks rise as their nostrils detected the scent of a dog.

Big dog. Bad dog. Worst-in-the-neighborhood dog. And a moment later a huge hairy mastiff came lumbering down the sidewalk, out for his evening stroll with his master.

Every cat in the parking lot dropped whatever he was eating. Backs arched, ears flattened, tails stiffened, claws clenched, throats hissed.

Bertram the Bad lunged toward the wall where the cat quartet had been sitting, and it was all his master could do to keep a tight rein on the leash.

"Bertram! Bad dog!" the master said.

The cats scattered like water on a hot skillet. In less than three seconds the wall behind the Fishmonger was empty, as bare as a cat's nose. The members of the Club of Mysteries went streaking down the alley, and it wasn't until Polo reached the stairs to the loft in Murphy's garage that he realized Marco was not with them. Neither was Texas Jake.

Polo, Boots, and Elvis turned and saw Texas coming slowly down the alley, leaning a little on Carlotta.

"That's right, lads. Just go off and leave me," Texas growled. "Just look out for your own tails and never mind the hindmost."

"Now, Texas, it's not like that," Boots told him. "We were just so startled that we ran without thinking."

"All you'd have to do is call and we'd come back for you," Elvis told him.

But Texas went on grumbling as he climbed the stairs.

"Who brought me little tidbits of food tonight? Who stayed with me in the alley? Carlotta, that's who." He reached the loft and hoisted himself up on the rocker. "All you lads are so busy figuring out who's going to take my place, you've no time to think of the cat who saved you from Bertram only a few weeks ago."

"We think of that all the time, Texas," Polo told him. "If it hadn't been for you, the rest of us would be hamburger now."

There was the soft sound of pawpads on the stairs, and suddenly Marco appeared, holding something large and pink in his mouth. He deposited his offering on the floor in front of Texas.

"For you," he said.

The big yellow cat with the white belly leaned forward. All the other cats gathered around to stare.

"What's this?" asked Texas Jake.

"A salmon?" said Marco hopefully. And then even *he* saw what he had grabbed in his haste. It was not a fish at all. It wasn't even a barbeque chicken leg. It was one of the cook's orange rubber scrub gloves, filled with garbage, smelling of fish.

Texas almost fell off the rocking chair laughing. The other cats joined in until the loft of Murphy's garage was filled with their raucous meows. Even Polo could not resist a snicker.

"I was in a hurry," Marco said, feeling foolish. "I saw the rest of you leaving, and gave it one last try."

"And you thought *you* might take my place, lad?" boomed Texas. "*You* could be Lord of the Loft? King of the Alley? Feline Commander and Cat Supreme? You make me laugh."

Marco slunk off into a corner and hunkered down, too embarrassed to speak. To make matters worse, he had spent so much time looking for a whole salmon for Texas Jake that he had not eaten a thing himself. His paws were dirty, his coat smelly, and right at that moment, he hated Texas Jake more than any other cat in the world.

4
CARLOTTA'S REQUEST

Long after the other cats settled down for the night, Marco lay with his head on one paw, listening to the snuffles and murmurs around him, accented now and then by the deep raggedy snore of Texas Jake.

As the soft pale light of the moon flooded the loft, however, he finally dozed off, but was awakened twice during the night. The first time he awoke to a soft thump, thump, thump on the floor, and opened one eye to see Texas Jake exercising his lame leg. Back and forth he walked, flexing his muscles, increasing his pace.

The next time, just after dawn, Marco awoke to the sound of a club meeting going on around him. It was not Texas Jake who was doing the talking, however; it was Carlotta. Texas appeared to be sleeping soundly in the rocker, but Marco noticed that every time anyone said, "Texas," the big cat's ears twitched.

"It would please me very much if every one of you thought about the best thing you could do for our noble, wounded leader," Carlotta was saying. "Surely there is one thing above all else that each of you could do that would restore Texas to health."

The silence in the loft was profound. Restoring Texas Jake to health was not foremost in the minds of the he-cats.

"It seems to me," Carlotta went on, "that the next leader of our club, if there *is* to be a new one, should be someone who truly cares about the Club of Mysteries. And if he truly cares about the club, then he cares about Texas and would do whatever he could to help him."

"But what?" asked Boots.

"Ah!" said Carlotta. "That's for you to decide. Let every cat give according to his strengths and talents."

"Well," said Elvis. "Since I am a singer, I shall compose a song in honor of Texas, to soothe his spirits and help him recover."

"Big deal," muttered Boots.

Elvis arched his back. "And what great contribution will *you* make?"

"I live by my wits and cleverness," said Boots. "I shall . . ." And here he thought long and hard. "*I* shall take a steak hot off my master's plate and bring it to Texas Jake to improve his strength," he said grandly.

"Very good," said Carlotta. "We will have a song—a very *long* song, I hope—to soothe Texas Jake's spirits, and a steak to restore his strength." She turned to Marco and Polo, who were up now, and stretching. "And what will our tabbies do to help?"

Marco wasn't sure, but he thought he saw one of Texas Jake's eyes open ever so slightly and close again.

Marco looked at Polo. What could they bring Texas that was even better than a steak or a song? What else did the big cat need, and what would prove them—Marco, in particular—the most able leader of all?

"Perhaps," said Marco finally, studying the big yellow cat sprawled there on the rocker, "we could find something that would help his wounds to heal."

Both of Texas Jake's ears twitched when Marco said those words, for medicine is the last thing on a cat's mind.

But Carlotta was impressed. "That is a fine idea!" she said. "I have heard that there is a plant called comfrey that is excellent to rub on wounds."

"What does it look like?" asked Polo.

"It has five little purple flowers on a stalk and leaves that grow first this way, then that way, all down the stem."

"That sounds easy enough," said Marco, wishing for a task a bit harder. "Where does it grow?"

"That's the problem," said Carlotta, looking anxious. "The only place I know is the city dump."

"So we'll go to the dump," Marco declared.

This time Carlotta's voice dropped. "Marco, that is where the Over-the-Hill Gang hangs out. You and Polo would be lucky to get out of there alive."

Marco wasn't certain, but he was almost sure he saw Texas Jake smile. Polo's legs, however, were shaking so badly that he thought he could hear the bones rattle.

"Well, my task is not exactly easy," said Elvis. "I have never composed a song longer than a verse or two."

29

"And if I steal a steak off my master's table, he could very well take me to the pound," said Boots.

"But if we go to the city dump, we may never be heard from again!" Polo breathed.

"You are all intelligent, clever, and brave," Carlotta said, licking each cat on the nose in turn. "I know you will do your best."

"Well, I'm off," said Elvis. "The true artist must have solitude in order to create." And he left.

"And I shall have to plan my act very carefully," said Boots. "It may not be today and it may not be tomorrow, but sometime soon I shall bring the meat off my master's table." Boots left also.

When only Marco and Polo remained, Carlotta went with them down the stairs to the alley below.

"Let me tell you about the Over-the-Hill Gang," she said. "Their leader is a short wiry tomcat called Steak Knife, and he is absolutely fearless. I am very fond of the two of you, and would hate to see anything happen."

"I am very fond of me too, and would hate to see anything happen," said Polo in a pitiful small voice. "I am so fond of myself, in fact, that I could easily go back to the Neals and spend the rest of my life in the velveteen basket."

"Polo, have you no pride?" Marco scolded. "Do you want the whole neighborhood to think we're cowards? Do you want the Persian, the Abyssinian, and the Siamese to gather at the Fishmonger and talk about how we wouldn't even try? We could never show our faces in the alley again."

"Would that be so bad?" Polo wondered aloud.

"There's more to life than security," Marco told him. "If you never take chances, what kind of a life is that?"

"A safe one," Polo replied.

"No," said Marco. "If all you want to do is lie in a velveteen basket, you may as well be a rock." He raised himself to his tallest height and held up his tail proudly. "If there is a comfrey plant that will help heal Texas Jake, then we will get it," he said.

"That's the spirit!" said Carlotta.

"But where *is* the dump?" asked Polo.

"Follow me," Carlotta told them.

They came to the Fishmonger at the end of the alley, and waited on the curb.

"You must be very, very careful when crossing this street," Carlotta said. "There is no excuse for a cat getting run over. If you look both ways, you will be all right. A flat cat is a dumb cat, we say here in the alley."

Once across the street, Carlotta took them down the alley on the other side. This was new territory, strange territory, with different sounds and smells. Polo wanted to stop and sniff each new trash can, each fence post, each box and brick, but Carlotta trotted on, the little bell on her collar giving off a faint tinkle.

The alley finally became a dirt path. A long path. Then the path became a field. Beyond the field were woods that rose far in the distance to become a hill.

"Do you see those trees?" asked Carlotta. "Do you see that hill?"

"Yes," said Marco and Polo.

"Beyond those trees and beyond that hill is the city dump. And in that dump is Steak Knife and his Over-the-Hill Gang. You might get through the trees and you might get up the hill, but the minute you go *over* the hill, you'll meet up with Steak Knife."

"And the comfrey?" Marco asked.

"I don't know," said Carlotta. "It's somewhere there in the dump." And she went back to Murphy's loft, leaving the tabbies on their own.

5
LOOKING FOR COMFREY

Marco had always assumed that Polo was the dumber of the two. Polo certainly acted stupid at times. What other cat would swallow twelve yards of Christmas ribbon and have to have a stomach operation?

But Polo suddenly opened his mouth and said something incredibly intelligent: "Maybe we can find the comfrey somewhere else."

Marco turned and looked at his brother. "Maybe we can."

They explored both sides of the path—around every bush—to see if just possibly, by the merest chance, there could be a plant with little purple flowers on a stalk and leaves growing first one way, then the other.

As they neared the trees, a scurrying sound in the dry October leaves caught their attention. Instantly Marco and

Polo crouched, bellies to the ground, ears alert, eyes wide, paws ready, their tails whipping back and forth.

Two small beady eyes looked out at them from a hole under a tree stump.

"Well, pounce if you're going to," squealed a small voice.

Marco's tail swished all the faster, and Polo's eyes grew as large and as dark as ripe olives.

"It speaks English," Polo whispered.

"The 'it' you refer to is a mouse," the voice said. "Timothy Mouse, Esquire, for your information."

Polo's tail stopped swishing. "What's the Esquire for?"

"How do I know?" said the mouse. "It's what my mother named me."

At the word "mother," Polo left his crouch position and simply lay down on his stomach, head on his paws. He was remembering something a long time ago called mother—something large and dark and warm and soft and smelling of milk and fur. Polo had no desire, really, to go looking for comfrey to heal Texas Jake. But if Marco ever suggested they look for their mother, Polo would have swum the widest river or climbed the highest mountain, just so he could smell that wonderful warm, soft, dark, milky, furry smell again.

"What did your mother name you?" came the squeak.

"She didn't name me anything. The Neals named me Polo," Polo told him.

"Why are you talking to him, Polo? He's a mouse," said Marco. "And mice are to be seen, not heard; eaten, not discussed."

"So eat me and get it over with," said Timothy Mouse, Esquire.

Marco's left paw shot out like lightning, but Timothy only scooted farther back under the stump.

"You need a longer paw," said the mouse, and sighed. "Where is it written that cats and mice can't be friends? We have names just like anyone else. You may call me Timothy."

Even Marco had to admire the small mouse. It was easy to think of eating a mouse, but different, somehow, to eat a Timothy.

Polo was still pondering the question. "I don't know why we can't be friends," he said at last.

"Great! Pleased to make your acquaintance then!" said Timothy. "What about your brother?"

"I haven't decided yet," said Marco.

Timothy's voice grew stronger. "You don't know what it's like to be chased every day of your life by an animal who just happens to be bigger than you. What are you tabbies doing out here so early in the morning anyway?"

"Looking for comfrey to heal Texas Jake," said Polo.

"The big yellow cat with the white belly?" asked Timothy. "Why do you want to help *him?* He's chased me more times than I can count."

"Well, he's brave when he has to be," said Marco. "Have you seen any comfrey?"

"I wouldn't know it from dandelions," Timothy told him. "But if there *is* such a plant, it's probably growing in the dump. There are weeds all over that place."

"That's what we were afraid of," Polo said. "Well, it was nice to meet you, Timothy. Consider yourself a friend."

"Thank you. And you, Marco?" the small mouse asked.

"I'm still thinking about it," Marco told him. "It's mostly reflex, you know. I see whiskers and a tail—especially the tail—and I pounce. Just like hiccups, I guess. My body goes on automatic."

"Then promise that if you *do* ever pounce on me, you'll let me go," Timothy pleaded.

"I think I could arrange to do that," Marco promised.

The cats went on then, the trees becoming thicker until there was no mistaking the fact that they were in the woods. They looked everywhere for comfrey—under rocks, behind tree stumps, in clumps of moss, along a brook. But there was no plant with little purple flowers on a single stalk, with leaves growing first one way and then the other. They would have to go to the dump.

Suddenly Polo stopped dead still, one paw in the air. Marco did the same.

They heard a hiss. Not a car. Not a snake. Not steam.

A hiss like only another cat can make. A wild hiss. An angry hiss. A get-out-of-our-woods kind of hiss that made their skins crawl, their backs arch, their tails thicken, and their claws clinch.

Two green eyes were looking at them from the bushes on the right.

Snap. Marco and Polo jerked around. Two green eyes were looking at them from the bushes on the left.

Suddenly the whole woods seemed alive with eyes and

hisses. A moment later Marco and Polo were running for their lives, back through the trees, along the path in the field, through the alley, and they didn't stop until they came to the street.

Polo leaned against his brother, panting, and glanced behind him.

The alley was empty. They were safe.

Once across the street and back on their own side, Polo had another thought. A brilliant thought. A surprisingly brilliant thought for a cat who would eat twelve yards of Christmas ribbon.

"Marco," he asked, "when do flowers bloom?"

"In the spring, stupid," Marco told him.

"Then why are we looking for a plant with purple flowers when this is fall and there are no flowers to be found?"

For the second time, Marco stopped and stared at his brother. "Polo, you astonish me! You are absolutely right! We are trying to do an impossible task, and will have to think of something else."

6
A LITTLE CONVERSATION

The loft was empty when the tabbies returned, so Marco and Polo settled down on a stack of old newspapers in the middle of the floor. They would have preferred the rocking chair, of course, but *no*body sat there except Texas Jake. Soon they fell fast asleep.

They awoke to find themselves in a patch of sunshine that came through the open window, and they stretched out on the dusty floorboards, Marco's head on Polo's belly. When the other members of the Club of Mysteries returned after a morning prowl around the neighborhood, they waited respectfully until Texas Jake arrived and climbed back up on his rocker, gently licking his stitches once he was settled.

"I am pleased to report that I have composed the first verse of a song for you, Texas," Elvis said, grooming one side of his long sleek body, then the other.

"Oh?" said Texas Jake. "Let me hear it!"

Elvis sat up straight, lifted his head, and sang:

> For he's a jolly good fe-line,
> For he's a jolly good fe-line,
> For he's a jolly good fe-line
> That nobody can deny.

Texas was not impressed. "It's been done," he said.

"What?" asked Elvis.

"It's been written already. You only changed one word."

"You said you were going to *compose* a song, Elvis, not copy one," Carlotta reminded him.

Elvis sulked. "It's *hard!*" he said.

"You wanted easy? You wanted simple? You wanted stupid?" asked Marco, beginning to hope that he, of all the cats, would prove yet to be the most able.

"If you think *your* task is hard, consider mine," Boots said. "I don't just have to steal a steak off my master's plate and somehow get it out the door. I have to wait until he *cooks* one, and there's not a thing I can do until he does, except look hopeful."

"That's the problem," said Carlotta, biting her claws. It was the one thing about her Marco did not like. Whenever she was the least bit nervous, she chewed her claws right down to the bone. He rather liked the dainty *tap, tap, tap* her claws made on the steps when she came up into the loft, but she was nervous now because she was afraid the cats would begin fighting among themselves again and forget their promise to help Texas.

"Humans simply can't communicate with us," she said. "When Master is cooking shrimp for dinner, I can sit by his chair and meow 'Please!' till Christmas, and he'll just reach down and scratch my head."

"And when you want to go out," said Marco, joining in, "why do they think you are sitting by the door meowing your head off? They'll walk right by as though they don't have an ear on their heads."

"Or Master forgets to change your litter. You complain and complain and he'll say, 'What's the matter with *you*, Elvis?' So I do my business on his rug, and then he gets upset."

"Have you ever noticed how angry they get when they find you drinking out of the toilet, even though they may not have changed the water in your bowl for a week?" asked Polo.

Texas Jake was getting interested in the conversation now. He hung over the edge of the rocker and looked down at the other cats with his great yellow eyes.

"The worst offender of all is the vet," he said, and immediately all the cats howled in agreement. When the noise had subsided, he went on: "A veterinarian has gone to medical school for the sole purpose of studying us and learning all that he can. He has felt us, smelled us, poked us, pulled us, and turned our ears inside out. Yet he still does not understand a word we say."

The cats yowled again, even louder.

"When I was taken to the vet after being mauled by Bertram the Bad, the first words out of my mouth were, 'Don't lay a hand on me.' So what did he do? Laid *both* hands on me." The fur on Texas Jake's neck bristled a little, as he remembered. "I put up a good fight, though. Took the vet and two technicians to hold me down."

"Just once," said Carlotta, her eyes snapping, "I would like to put *my* master in a house controlled by cats and see how *he* likes it. 'Feed me!' he'd beg, and I'd just reach down and scratch his head."

It was a most appealing idea, and the cats all sprawled out, one head on the belly of the cat next to him, enjoying the picture Carlotta had painted.

"If he said, 'Open the door,' I'd ask, 'What are *you* yowling about?'" Marco told them.

"I'd never flush his toilet, and if he did his business on my rug, I'd say, 'Baaaad Master! Bad! Bad! Bad!'" said Elvis.

"If he got out and wanted back in, he could sit outside the window and howl his head off before I'd open the door again," added Boots.

"And if he wanted a glass of water, I'd give him a cracker or a pickle instead—anything except what he really wanted—just to see how *he* liked it!" said Polo.

They all looked at Texas Jake.

"If he ever looked the least bit sleepy," Texas said, "I'd pick him up and say, 'Here, Master. You look a little sick. Let me take your temperature.'"

"Yes, yes, yes!" the cats all screeched, and Marco had never heard such a commotion.

When the noise died down, Texas Jake leaned back and studied the cats before him. "I thought you lads had volunteered to do a little something to make me better. So what was I hearing a minute ago? Complaints, that's what. Boots was complaining, Elvis was complaining. What *are* we, a club of whiners? What do you tabbies want to complain about?"

"Nothing at all," said Marco. "But I'd like to make a small observation, if I may. Polo and I wanted to find something that would make your wounds heal faster, and Carlotta suggested comfrey—a plant with purple flowers on a single stem, the leaves growing first this way and then that. But it seems we overlooked one small detail. Flowers bloom in spring, and this is fall. There are no purple flowers anywhere in sight. So if you can think of another plant that might heal your wounds, Polo and I would be most happy to oblige."

But Carlotta walked across the loft and rubbed their noses. "My dear friends," she said. "You will simply have to find comfrey *without* its flowers, that's all."

Marco let out his breath. Polo felt weak in the knees. It would take even longer to find the plant without the flowers, which meant they would be in the dump for a long time, meaning they would most certainly be spotted by Steak Knife and his Over-the-Hill Gang, which meant that Marco and Polo would probably never get out alive.

There was a grin on Texas Jake's face, and his eyes became little yellow slits of sheer delight.

"Does that make you happy, Texas?" Marco asked bluntly. "That out of the goodness of our hearts we have volunteered to hunt for comfrey and risk our very lives? Why, may I ask, don't you like us?"

Texas Jake's eyes opened wide. "My good fellow, why would I not like you? Just because Marco goes around bragging about how he can *reeead*? Just because Polo makes eyes at Carlotta? Just because you tabbies, who are still house cats if I ever saw them, come waltzing up here to the loft as though you are full-fledged members, and Marco even talks about taking over my position as Cat Supreme, is that any reason for me not to *like* you?"

As far as Marco was concerned, those were four good reasons right there.

"No, indeed," Texas went on. "I know good fellows when I see them. I heard you tell Carlotta that you wanted to find something that would make my wounds heal, and I could tell right away you didn't want a quick assignment, a simple any-fool-can-do-it job. You want to be tried! You want to be tested! You want to show old Texas what tabbies like you are made of!"

Texas Jake's tail was swishing back and forth now as he spoke. "No, sir, I knew you wanted to do something worthy of your bravery and courage."

And just the way he said it, Marco and Polo knew there was no turning back. Somewhere over there in the dump was the comfrey, and somewhere, near the comfrey, was Steak Knife and his gang.

7
DETECTIVE WORK

W hat are we going to do, Marco?" Polo meowed softly
after the other cats had taken their usual places in the loft
and were blissfully napping.

"Detective work," Marco answered. "Find out all we
can about Steak Knife and the Over-the-Hill Gang. If we
absolutely have to go to the dump to get the comfrey, then
we have to know what we're up against."

"We could still go back to the Neals'," Polo reminded
him. "There would be food in our porcelain bowl, water in
our dish, a velveteen basket to curl up in at night, and
someone to scratch our ears."

"First things first," said Marco. "First we get the comfrey for Texas, *then* we go back to the Neals'."

Polo got up slowly and stretched so far that his rump
went way up in the air and his chest touched the floor. And

then, with one last look at Carlotta, he followed Marco out of the loft, down the stairs, and into the alley below.

They had not gone ten feet when suddenly Marco's body made a leap, a huge leap—a gray cannonball of fur—that was followed by a startled squeal.

"Timothy!" cried Polo. And sure enough, when Marco's body came to rest, he had the tiny mouse trapped between his paws.

Marco looked at Timothy. Timothy looked at Marco.

Swish, swish went Marco's tail.

Timothy didn't move a whisker.

"To eat or not to eat," Marco pondered.

"Not to eat," suggested Timothy.

And just when Marco wondered how a small tender ear would taste, he remembered that the ear had a name, and let him go.

"You remembered," said Timothy. "Thank you very much."

"What are you doing over here?" asked Polo. "I thought you lived in the woods."

"I get around," Timothy answered. "The whole neighborhood is my home."

"Then tell us what you know about a cat named Steak Knife," said Marco.

At the very mention of the name, Timothy began to tremble. His whiskers drooped, his paws quivered, and his tail curled between his legs.

"Then you know him?" asked Polo.

"The meanest, baddest cat in town," said Timothy. "I came within a whisker of becoming his lunch."

"What can you tell us about him?" Marco asked. "We can't get the comfrey without running into Steak Knife."

"I can tell you one thing," said Timothy. "He's a collector."

"Stamps?" asked Polo. "Buttons? Matchbook covers? String?"

Timothy shook his head. "Tails."

Marco and Polo froze.

"T-tails?" Polo repeated.

"Mouse tails, rat tails, bird tails, cat tails . . . He's got them hanging over the fence down at the city dump. And now, if you'll excuse me . . ." And like a streak, Timothy was gone.

Polo looked at his brother. "*Cat* tails? Marco, listen, the Neals probably miss us! We can *still* go back home."

And when Marco started off in the opposite direction, Polo said plaintively, "I *like* my tail, Marco! I've always liked my tail, and I'd like to keep it a long time. I don't want it hanging over a fence at the city dump."

"The way to keep our tails is to keep our wits about us," Marco told him. "Come on."

They went up the alley to the Fishmonger to see if there just might be any trout fillets lying around. There weren't, but there *were* a few half-eaten sardines in the trash can. After Marco and Polo had filled themselves, they came up out of the garbage to see the Abyssinian dining not ten feet away.

"Good afternoon," said Marco. "And a lovely day it is."

The Abyssinian *never* looked as though the day were lovely, however, and only grunted as he scarfed down a piece of bacon.

"May I ask you a question?" Marco said. "How long have you lived in the neighborhood?"

"Twelve years, going on thirteen," the Abyssinian told Marco, wiping one paw over his nose and licking his chops.

"May I assume, then, that you know every cat in town?"

"Except for a new kitten here and there, I suppose I do," the Abyssinian said.

"Then what is the first thing that comes to mind when I mention the name Steak Knife?" Marco asked.

"Thunder, lightning, and hailstorms," the Abyssinian answered. "You cats wouldn't be out looking for trouble, would you?"

"We'd like nothing better than *never* meeting up with

48

Steak Knife, but I'm afraid we must," said Marco, and they set off once again.

Across the parking lot, a large crow was pecking at a piece of pork chop that it had scavenged from the trash.

"*Caw! Caw!* Go 'way, go 'way!" the crow cawed as the tabbies came closer.

"Relax," said Marco, "we don't want your pork chop, just your advice."

The crow stopped pecking and paused with one leg raised, his head cocked to the left. He looked as though he rather liked giving advice.

"You've been around," said Marco. "You've seen the country from above, below, and sideways. There's probably not a thing you miss."

"Not much," said the crow.

"We're looking for a cat named Steak Knife. How will we know him when we see him?"

The crow cocked his head to the other side. "Look for two beady eyes, a long slithery body, sharp jagged claws, raggedy white fur with black spots, mange on the hind quarters, and a scar over the right eye. That's Steak Knife."

Polo could feel his heart thumping against his rib cage.

"Do you know what will happen if you go near the dump?" asked the crow. "Do you know what will happen if you find Steak Knife? I will be flying around some morning and I will see two gray lumps lying in the road—like clumps of wet leaves. I'll fly down to investigate, and it will be you, that's what. What is left of you. I will pause, of course, for a moment of silent meditation, and then all my friends and I shall pick the meat off your bones and bid you adieu."

Now Polo was trembling so violently that his ears shook. "Maybe we could get to the dump by another route," he said. "Maybe they wouldn't be expecting us if we came another way."

"On the other side of the dump is the river," the crow said. "Unless you can swim, this path is your only route. And *nobody* goes through the woods and the dump without meeting up with Steak Knife and his gang. Good-bye, tasty gray lumps." And he was off, the piece of pork chop in his mouth.

8
ODE TO TEXAS JAKE

There didn't seem to be much point in going after the comfrey that very minute, not if twenty-four hours later their bones would be picked clean by the crows. And besides, the other cats should be arriving at the Fishmonger any minute now, so why hurry off? Marco thought. If there was food to be had, why face death this minute?

Indeed, Boots and Elvis were coming down the alley already, followed by Carlotta and Texas Jake, who still limped rather badly. The Persian and the Siamese were arriving from the other direction, and a few moments later, everyone was there. Cats sat all along the back wall, on top of garbage cans, and even on the hoods of cars.

"Big excitement!" Carlotta told the tabbies. "Elvis has finished the song he wrote for Texas Jake, and will be singing it for us soon."

"See?" Polo said to Carlotta. "Elvis chose such an easy job that he's finished already."

"Composing is harder than you think," Carlotta told him.

"I could do it in a minute," Polo bragged.

"Just try," said Carlotta.

Polo cleared his throat and said:

> Oh, Texas Jake
> Is like a . . . uh . . . snake.

"What?" said Texas, looking down from the highest trash can where he had taken the place of honor.

"I was just practicing rhymes," Polo said quickly.

"Hush," said Carlotta. "Elvis is about to sing."

Indeed, the sleek black cat was already preening himself on the wall. His long pink tongue reached up to his nose, then halfway down each whisker.

When he was quite sure that all were paying attention, he gave his whiskers one last tweak. "Ode to Texas Jake," he said, and began the song to the tune of "Camptown Races."

> Texas Jake is quite a cat,
> Doo dah, doo dah,
> Only one to catch a rat,
> Oh, doo dah day.

"Stop right there," said Texas.

Elvis looked around.

"What's this 'doo dah' business? I rescue kittens, save

felines, fight off rabid squirrels and Bertram the Bad, and all I get is a 'doo dah day'?"

"But, Texas, it's the song! That's just the way it goes," Elvis explained.

"Well, make it go somewhere else," Texas told him.

Elvis looked hopelessly about him, but Carlotta, as always, came to the rescue.

"Oh, Texas, don't be so modest," she purred. "I *know* that 'doo dahs' and 'doo dah days' are reserved for kings and dignitaries, but *surely*, with all you've done for us and the Club of Mysteries, you are King of the Alley. Please let Elvis keep his 'doo dahs.'"

The Siamese tried to be helpful. "When you go to see the king, you always bow down on one knee and say, 'Doo dah, your majesty,'" he said.

"Or," added the Persian, "if he is an *extremely* important king, you say, 'Doo dah *day*, your majesty!'"

"Is that so?" said Texas. "Well, then, let's hear the next verse."

Elvis opened his mouth once again and tipped back his head:

> Was he frightened? Not at all.
> Doo dah, doo dah,
> Texas Jake is ten feet tall,
> Oh, doo dah day.
>
> Gonna sing all night,
> Gonna sing all day.

> 'Bout a dude named Texas Jake,
> Don't get in his way.

Polo was envious of a cat who could compose songs. And as the black cat went on, he wondered why his *own* meows didn't sound as good as Elvis's, why his *own* body didn't jiggle and sway the way Elvis's did when *he* sang:

> See him comin' down the street,
> Doo dah, doo dah,
> Runnin' on his padded feet,
> Oh, doo dah day!
>
> Call your kittens! Show your wives!
> Doo dah, doo dah,
> Here's a cat who has nine lives!
> Oh, doo dah day!
>
> Gonna sing all night,
> Gonna sing all day.
> 'Bout a dude named Texas Jake,
> Don't get in his way.

Texas stopped him again. "You already sang that part."

"That's the chorus," Elvis explained. "After each verse, you repeat the chorus."

"Oh," said Texas. "Then you may proceed."

> Bertram Bad come up the stairs,
> Doo dah, doo dah,

Texas grab him by the ears,
Oh, doo dah day.

Bertram toss him on the floor,
Doo dah, doo dah,
Texas jump up, ask for more,
Oh, doo dah day.

Gonna sing all night,
Gonna sing all day.
'Bout a dude named Texas Jake,
Don't get in his way.

Texas's head seemed to be getting bigger and bigger the longer the song went on:

Think he's dyin', think he's gone,
Doo dah, doo dah,
Texas Jake goes on and on,
Oh, doo dah day.

Plan his funeral, that's a laugh,
Doo dah, doo dah,
Texas Jake not dead by half,
Oh, doo dah day.

Gonna sing all night,
Gonna sing all day.
'Bout a dude named Texas Jake,
Don't get in his way.

Watch the alley clear out fast,
Doo dah, doo dah,
Texas comin', he come last,
Oh, doo dah day.

He-cats fear his angry stare,
Doo dah, doo dah,
She-cats love his yellow hair,
Oh, doo dah day.

Gonna sing all night,
Gonna sing all day.
'Bout a dude named Texas Jake,
Don't get in his way.

Finally, Elvis sang the last verse, and when he got to the chorus the Siamese, the Persian, and the Abyssinian joined in:

King of Alley, Cat Supreme,
Doo dah, doo dah,
Chief Commander, Cream of Cream,
Oh, doo dah day.

Raise your voices, lift your ears,
Doo dah, doo dah,
Texas Jake gets fifty cheers,
Oh, doo dah day.

Gonna sing all night,
Gonna sing all day.

'Bout a dude named Texas Jake,
Don't get in his way.

The song was over, and all the cats began to yowl together to show their appreciation. But in the midst of all the rejoicing, one voice sounded loud and clear: "I don't!"

All the cats turned to see Marco standing stiffly beneath the wall, facing Texas on the trash can.

Texas Jake leaned over and studied him with beady eyes. "You don't what?"

"Don't fear you, Texas."

The other cats gathered around to see what would happen next.

"Oh, don't you, now?" asked Texas Jake.

"No. I respect you and admire you for saving the Club of Mysteries from Bertram the Bad, but I don't shiver when I see you coming or shake when I hear your voice or quiver when you give me your angry stare."

Polo was speechless with fright. He had never heard his brother talk so big or act so bold. Maybe, because he figured he was going to die anyway, Marco decided he might as well say what he thought.

"Hadn't you better apologize to Texas?" Carlotta hissed softly.

But Texas just raised himself up a little higher on the trash can and said, with a loud meow, "Should he apologize? No, indeed! Let the cat be! He was only speaking his mind. Obviously, Marco is a cat of *learning*. Marco, after all, can *reeead*! A cat of Marco's intelligence will

soon be back with the comfrey he has promised. Isn't that right, Marco?"

"Right," the tabby replied.

Polo decided that the city dump where the comfrey grew had never seemed so far, and death so near, as it did just then.

9
A KINGDOM OF CATS

It began to rain then, much to Polo's relief, because not even Texas would expect a cat to go out in the rain. The two tabbies returned to the loft with the others and lay down on the floor to digest their meal.

Boots seemed nervous that Elvis had won such favor from Texas Jake, and that the big cat might select the singer to be the next Lord of the Alley, Cat Supreme. So he said, "I happen to know that my master is having a special dinner on Friday night. He has invited a lady, of whom he is very fond, for a steak dinner by candlelight. You can expect your steak then, Texas."

"Very good!" said the yellow cat. "I will look forward to it."

Boots rolled over on his back, paws in the air and said, "Think how much easier it would be, though, if I were a garbageman. I'd just empty the trash cans outside the steak house, and as soon as I found a half-eaten sirloin, I'd rush it to you. No more hanging around, waiting for my master to invite his lady love to dinner."

All the cats pricked up their ears and listened.

"Not me," said Elvis. "I wouldn't be a garbageman. If I were a human, I'd be a butcher. Why settle for a steak somebody else has chewed? A butcher can eat anything he likes. I'd have kidney pie for breakfast, a little sausage for lunch, and fillet of salmon with catnip sauce for dinner."

"I would choose to be a cleaning lady," said Carlotta. "Can you imagine what it would be like to run the vacuum nozzle right up against my master's ankles and say, 'Move it, buster!'"

"If I could be anything I liked, I'd be a doorman," said Polo dreamily. "I'd spend my life opening all the doors I can't open now. Get a little hungry? Open a door. Want to go outside? Open a door. All day long I'd open doors."

"You're out of your minds," said Marco. "There is only one job that any self-respecting cat should want, and that is the job of dogcatcher."

"Yes! Yes!" cried Carlotta, Polo, Boots, and Elvis.

"Imagine the joy of running down the street with a net and rounding up all our enemies! Of putting Bertram the Bad in the back of a paddy wagon and carting him off to the pound! What ecstasy! What delight! The greatest job in the world!"

The cats began to meow and cheer again, but suddenly a deep growl rose above the shouting:

"Wrong! Wrong! Wrong!"

All the cats turned to the rocking chair to see Texas looking down on them with a fierce scowl.

"Do my ears deceive me?" he thundered. "You could choose anything at all, and you choose to be a garbageman? A butcher? A cleaning lady? A doorman or dogcatcher? Have you no backbones? Have you no spines? Dogcatcher, indeed! Why do you allow yourselves to be flim-flammed by a second-rate cat who thinks he knows it all? Set your sights high! What is the highest post a human can attain?"

Marco looked around sheepishly. With all his reading he should certainly know, but he just couldn't think. Policeman? Fireman?

"King! King of the World!" said Texas Jake. "A king is Commander in Chief and His Royal Highness all rolled up into one."

"Who is King of the World now?" asked Polo timidly.

"Why, the mayor!" said Texas. "The mayor is King of the World."

He certainly knew a great deal, Marco decided, for a cat who couldn't read.

"The King can tell you what time to get up in the morning and when to go to bed at night. When to clip your claws or clean your ears. He could order all dogs executed at dawn, and appoint all cats to his cabinet."

He himself was doomed, Marco decided. Despite all his learning, he had never known that the mayor was King of the World and that he had the power to order all dogs executed at dawn.

The cats maintained a respectful silence until Boots

asked finally, "If you were king, Texas, what laws would you make?"

Texas leaned back in the rocker, letting his tail hang over the edge. "Well, it would be a democracy, of course! Every cat would be equal to every other cat regardless of color, size, spots, or stripes. No *dogs*, mind you. And of course squirrels, rats, and other riffraff couldn't vote, but it would be a land of opportunity, with liberty and justice for cats."

"And if you were king, would you have elections?"

"Absolutely! If the cats voted for someone strong and intelligent—like me, for example—then I would simply remain king. But if they voted for just any fool who came along—some new cat in the neighborhood, say, who thought he was so clever, so smart, just because he could *reeead* . . ." And here Texas let his meow hang in the air like clothes on a line, "Then I'd have no choice but to declare the election null and void. Over and done with. Out with the morning trash. And I'd have to go on being king till the cats came to their senses."

Marco felt his muscles begin to tense, but it was Carlotta who spoke. "That doesn't seem quite fair, Texas."

Texas reared back in his chair. "Fair? *Fair?* Carlotta, my dear, a *king* decides what is fair. If I say it is fair, it is fair. If I say night is day, it is day. My word is law."

"And if some cat says it isn't?" asked Marco boldly, the hair on his back beginning to rise.

"Then I would have him thrown to the dogs," growled Texas.

There was no greater insult to a cat than that. Marco could not stop himself. He lunged at Texas, aiming for the scruff of the neck, and as soon as his teeth sank into flesh, he felt Texas Jake's old yellow teeth gripping the skin on his foreleg.

Around and around they went, until Marco's gray fur and Texas Jake's yellow fur became a gold and silver blur. Tufts of hair flew here, flew there. The loft was filled with the hideous sound of their cries and hisses.

Polo crawled under the army cot, sure that he was witnessing the end of his tabby brother.

Carlotta was meowing, "No! No! No!" But Boots and Elvis simply watched in fascination with narrowed eyes, waiting to see who the victor would be. This had never happened before in the Club of Mysteries.

Marco had been so angry he couldn't even think. His muscles, teeth, and claws spoke for him, but a few seconds into the fight, he realized he had made perhaps the biggest mistake of his life. He had attacked the Commander in Chief, the Cat Supreme, the Lord of the Loft, and the King of the Alley himself! And then another thought that made him suddenly retract his claws, unlock his teeth, and roll backward.

He had attacked an *injured* cat. Surely there was no mistake worse than that.

As each cat regained his breath and the shrieking and hissing stopped, a huge great silence filled the loft.

Carlotta spoke first, "Marco, you should be ashamed!"

Oh, he was ashamed. He was truly and deeply ashamed

that he had let his anger get the best of him. And so Marco did what only the strong can do: He apologized.

"I ask your pardon," he said to Texas. "And I hope I did not hurt you. In a moment of anger, I lost my head. I should never have attacked."

Texas did not answer right away. He was licking his scratches, and seemed to be thinking it over. Finally he said in his deep voice, "There are two reasons to bring me comfrey now, my lad—for my old wounds and for my fresh ones."

"I won't come back without it," said Marco, and went out into the rain, Polo behind him.

10
STEAK KNIFE

Shut up," said Marco, even before Polo said one word.

"I may be stupid, Marco, but I'd never do anything like that," Polo answered.

"Don't remind me."

"You must have been out of your head."

"I have never done anything like that in my life," said Marco, "but *somebody* has to show up that big yellow air bag and take him down a notch or two. Democracy indeed! Elections, my paw!"

"But who will respect you now?"

"I will simply have to prove myself, Polo. I will have to be stronger, smarter, and more fair in every way than Texas Jake, and the only way to do that is for us to outwit Steak Knife and come back with the comfrey."

Something was a bit wrong here, Polo thought. Together, he and Marco had to risk their very tails, yet it was Marco who would do the proving. But he followed along, faithful as always.

There was almost no traffic at the end of the alley by the Fishmonger, but Marco and Polo looked both ways, as Carlotta had taught them. Then they crossed the street and went up the alley on and on until it became a dirt path in a field. They slunk along on their bellies in the tall grass, toward the hill that loomed in the distance and the trees that covered it.

When they reached the woods, though it was not yet dark, it seemed night. There were shadows in the thick trees; deep piles of rotting leaves and branches; and many scurryings, rustlings, and eyes.

Eyes here. Eyes there. Green eyes, yellow eyes . . . The eyes moved when Marco and Polo moved, stopped when the cat brothers stopped.

"M-Marco!" Polo mewed, his paws trembling. "Do you s-see what I see?"

"Just keep walking like we own the place," Marco told him.

But as they passed a hollow log, a voice inside it called, "Who goes there?"

Polo leaped at least eight inches off the ground.

"Marco and Polo," Marco replied, making his voice as bold and brave sounding as he could, though his heart was pounding hard in his chest.

"This hill belongs to the Over-the-Hill Gang. Go back where you came from," the voice in the log hissed.

"We will as soon as we get what we came for," said Marco, and Polo felt sicker by the minute.

At this, all of the eyes seemed to move closer—from every stump, every clump, every bush, every branch—peering out from behind every tree.

There was a rustling, scuttling noise inside the log. Two dirty white ears appeared, followed by a nose, four dirty white paws, and a coal black tail.

It was the raggediest, scraggliest cat Marco and Polo had ever seen—a cat that seemed not to have been cleaned or combed for its entire life. Its hair was missing in places, one ear was torn, and he appeared to be blind in one eye. At the very sight of the scruffy creature, Polo felt his hair stand on end, his tail grow thick, his eyes grow large, his claws clench, and a high whine came from the back of his throat.

Marco and the raggedy, scraggly cat faced off.

"And what are you after?" the raggedy cat questioned.

"A friend of ours has been wounded and needs some comfrey that grows in the dump," Marco told him.

The raggedy cat looked hard at Marco. "That wouldn't be old Texas, would it? Big yellow cat with a white belly?"

"Yes, that's the cat," said Marco, determined to tell it straight out, fight if he must. "He had a run-in with Bertram the Bad and needs the comfrey to help his wounds heal faster."

"Indeed!" said the dirty white cat with the black tail. "Does he, now? What a coincidence!"

"A coincidence?" asked Marco, surprised that the scruffy animal had not attacked him already.

"It's a coincidence that just this morning I passed some comfrey right over the top of the hill. I know where to find it, and if you will allow me, I will take you to it. Steak Knife at your service."

At the name Steak Knife, Marco's fur rose straight up in the air, but still the dirty white cat did not budge.

"Ah, yes, I know that old rascal. Texas is Commander in Chief of some club or other, isn't he?" Steak Knife went on. "A right good fighter he is. A cat like that *deserves* to be healed, mate."

Polo could not believe his ears.

"I thought you and Texas were enemies," he said.

"Enemies we may be, but a fighter like Texas gets respect," said Steak Knife. "Follow me and I'll show you right where the comfrey grows." At that the green and yellow eyes became a tattered crew of cats, inching out of the bushes until they had the tabbies surrounded.

"M-Marco!" Polo whispered. "I don't think we should go. It's a trap! They'll lure us into the dump and bury us alive!"

Steak Knife overheard.

"You doubt me?" he asked. "Did you come here to fight? Did you come here to steal? No, indeed, you came on a mission of mercy, and you may take the comfrey back to Texas Jake with my compliments."

This was too easy! Marco and Polo began to feel better. Perhaps Steak Knife's reputation was worse than his bite.

When they all reached the top of the hill and came out of the trees, Marco saw the dump lying below them. Beyond the dump was a second hill, and beyond that, the river.

They moved along the rim of the hill, noses to the ground—Steak Knife, then Marco, then Polo, then the raggle-taggle crew of cats behind. In and around trees they meandered, over logs and stumps.

Finally Steak Knife paused and looked about him.

"Now," he said, "we are looking for a tall plant with a hairy stem, and the leaves point first one way, then the other."

"Right," said Marco.

The raggle-tailed cat led them through the weeds that were growing taller and thicker all the time, and Marco's heart thumped harder and harder.

"Marco!" Polo bleated again. "There are cats in front of us, cats beside us, cats behind us. Let's make a break while we still have a chance."

Marco himself cast a sidelong glance at the Over-the-Hill Gang. But suddenly Steak Knife's voice came again just ahead of them, "Here we are. A nice little patch of comfrey. Take what you need, my friends, and give that old yellow cat my regards."

"You are more generous than I expected," said Marco.

"Not at all! Not at all! He'd do the same for me, mates. Guarantee you that."

So Marco pulled up one of the plants with his teeth, Polo pulled up another, scarcely believing their good luck. Holding the stems securely, careful not to mangle the leaves, they made their way back down the hill, through the trees, and finally they were heading down the path that became an alley. They crossed the street by the Fishmonger and ran up the steps of Murphy's loft, where the other cats were settling down for the night.

The other members of the Club of Mysteries stopped and stared as Marco and Polo came across the floor and laid the plants before Texas Jake.

"Comfrey," said Marco. "To rub on your wounds and help them heal."

The big yellow cat's eyes opened wide. He inched forward on the rocker and hung over the edge, his nose working up and down.

Suddenly the hair on his neck began to rise, his back arched, and a low deep growl came roaring up out of his throat, ending with a hiss.

"Foxglove!" he meowed loudly. "You have brought me foxglove, not comfrey! You think I'm a fool?" He turned to Boots and Elvis. "They're trying to kill me, lads. Foxglove's a deadly poison."

11
TRAITORS!

There was absolute silence in the loft. If there had been a clock, you might have heard it ticking, but there was nothing.

And then, low at first, but growing louder, then louder still, came a hissing sound. Backs began to arch, fur to rise, tails to thicken, throats to growl.

"Poison?" Carlotta cried. "Marco, how *could* you?"

"Poison!" hissed Boots. "Traitors in our midst."

"And you know what we do to traitors!" said Elvis, his claws gleaming in the moonlight.

Texas Jake rose to a full standing position on the rocker. "They were trying to do away with me, lads!" he said reproachfully.

"We weren't!" Polo declared.

"We thought it was comfrey!" said Marco. "It has a tall stem, and leaves that grow first one way, then another!"

The cats ignored him.

"What *do* we do to traitors?" Boots asked. "Turn them over to Bertram the Bad?"

"But he *said* it was comfrey!" Polo insisted loudly.

All the cats spoke together. "*Who* said?"

"Steak Knife," Marco told them, realizing it had been a trick.

Again a terrible hiss filled the loft.

"Sssssteak Knife!"

"You *saw* him?" cried Carlotta.

"You *met* him?" asked Boots.

"You *talked* with him?" asked Elvis.

"You *plotted* with him!" growled Texas.

"No!" said Marco. "I swear it. You wanted comfrey, and it grows in the dump. We all know that Steak Knife and his gang own the dump."

"We could see their eyes watching," Polo put in.

"I was determined to get the comfrey, no matter what the cost," Marco continued, and he sounded a bit grand. "I would fight to the death if necessary to win your respect once again."

"So when we saw this raggedy, scraggly cat, who asked why we were there . . . ," Polo said, now wanting to be a part of the story.

"I told him what we were there for, and he said he would help," finished Marco.

The cats groaned in unison.

"How could you be so stupid?" asked Boots.

"I *was* stupid," Marco confessed. "But he told me that even though you were enemies, T. J., he had the highest regard for you. A real fighter, he said, that's you."

74

Texas Jake's tail stopped swishing and his ears perked up. "*He* said that about me?"

"Yes, indeed," said Marco. "He said he would be honored to help me find some comfrey, and that I should deliver it to you with his compliments."

"And look what he *sent!*" growled Texas. "Poison!"

"He said you'd do the same for him," Polo mewed. "He said that a fighter as great as you deserved to have his wounds healed. We were taken in with his words, and should have suspected, but anyone could have been fooled."

"That's true," Carlotta said, eager to have the quarrel between Texas and Marco resolved. "Everything Steak Knife said about you was true, Texas, so why wouldn't they believe he was really giving them comfrey? What would they know about foxglove?"

Carlotta's voice had a soothing effect, and finally Texas said, "Well, cats as stupid as these can't be expected to tell comfrey from foxglove. We can't all be smart, I guess."

Marco suppressed a growl and tried to look humble, but he was only angrier still at Texas and the way he had been humiliated in front of the others. Soon the cats were pawing at their bedding once again, preparing to lie down. And when Texas began to lick his fur and rub his ears with one paw, Polo knew the worst was over and that, for now anyway, they were safe.

Wearily Marco lay down beside Polo and closed his eyes. And perhaps because they appeared to be sleeping, Carlotta began whispering about them as the others settled down for the night.

"Texas," she mewed, "Marco and Polo really did risk their lives for you. If they go back to the dump, we will probably never see them again, you know."

"Would that be so bad?" Texas said.

"I'd sort of miss the stupid one," said Boots. "A cat who chases his tail when he doesn't have anything else to do is simply not playing with a full deck, in my opinion. He's a little empty between the ears."

"That's true," said Elvis. "A cat can always *sleep*, after all. Why waste energy chasing your tail?"

It was all Polo could do not to reach over and bite one of them.

"I'd sort of miss Marco," Elvis said. "It *is* handy to have a cat around who can read 'Wet Paint', for example, or 'Dangerous Crossing' or 'Beware of the Dog.'"

"Cats don't *need* to read," growled Texas. "We can *smell* wet paint. We can *see* that a crossing is dangerous, and you can certainly hear a dog. That humans need signs only proves that cats are smarter than people. Humans, my friends, have the most useless ears, eyes, and noses of any living creature I know."

"But if that's true, Texas—if they are so stupid—why do they live in houses and drive cars, while we cats have to depend on them?" meowed Carlotta.

"My dear, dear Carlotta," said Texas, "humans live in houses because they have no *fur*. The poor naked things would freeze to death if they had no houses. They need cars because their legs are so weak and wobbly they cannot do very much with them. Have you ever in your life seen your master leap from floor to table to bookcase? Of course not!"

The other cats were silent for a while, thinking it over, but then Boots spoke up, "But who *makes* the cars and houses?"

"Yes, yes!" cried the other cats. "If humans are so stupid, where do their clothes and cars and houses come from?"

Again there was a pause. This time Marco did not think he could stand it. It was all he could do to keep himself from saying the answer. But once again Texas Jake knew things that even Marco did not know.

"My dear friends," he said softly, almost sadly. "I cannot believe my own ears. I thought that the Club of Mysteries had solved such problems long ago. Do you not use your eyes? Your ears? Clothes come from stores, cars come from trucks, and houses grow right out of the ground."

It was almost frightening to be in the presence of such intelligence, Polo decided.

"Have you never noticed," Texas went on, "that when someone opens the door of a shop over on the boulevard, all you see are clothes? And have you never heard the sound of a huge truck coming through the intersection with its insides showing, and what do we see? *Cars,* my friends! Rows of cars! A litter of cars! Trucks give birth to cars just as cats have kittens."

Polo felt quite sure that if he stayed in the Club of Mysteries long enough, he would be almost as smart as Texas Jake.

"As for houses," the big yellow cat went on, "do you remember the big empty lot next to the gas station? One week we walked by and it was still empty—as naked as a cat's nose. The next week there was a house on it! It hadn't finished growing yet, by any means, but there it was, popping right up out of the earth."

This time a long profound silence settled over the loft. It was only Carlotta who dared break it. "But Texas," she purred softly, "if cats are so smart and humans so stupid, why is it that they are our masters?"

Ha! thought Marco. I wonder if Texas has an answer for that. He opened one eye to see if the big cat looked the least bit uncomfortable. The loft, however, was dark and Marco could only make out the shape of Texas's large head up on the rocker.

"Two little things," said Texas. "Only two little things make humans our masters: a thumb and a finger."

"What's so great about that?" asked Elvis. "We've got pawpads and claws."

"Indeed, but can you press one claw against another? A human, my friends, can bring the thumb and the finger together. Cats cannot."

From where he lay on the pile of newspapers, Marco tried. He could not. Polo tried too. Neither could bring two of their claws together. From the rustlings in the dark of the loft, the tabbies could tell that all the cats were trying it out.

"You're right," said Boots. "We can't, but so what?"

"So what? So *what?*" said Texas sadly. "It means that humans can button their own clothes. They can feed themselves with a spoon and not have to get down on all fours to eat. It means that they can write with a pencil and cook a dinner and drive a car and open a door."

"Then we shall never be masters," sighed Carlotta.

"My dear, you are wrong," Texas told her. "Answer this: Who fills your water dish?"

"Humans," said Carlotta.

"Who gives you your breakfast and dinner?"

"Humans," said Boots.

"Who cleans your litter box, combs your fur, drives you to the vet, and opens doors for you, coming and going?"

"Humans," said Carlotta.

"So who are the real masters? Cats, of course, and humans are merely our servants."

At the mention of "master," however, Boots remembered his promise, and gave a loud sigh.

"Tomorrow is Friday," he said, "and you know what happens on Friday."

"Yes, you bring me a steak," said Texas eagerly.

Polo was very glad to hear it. Misery does love company, and Polo really wanted company. He wanted to know that at least one other cat in the Club of Mysteries had offered to do something even half as difficult as the task he and Marco had agreed to do.

The cats all bedded down for a good long sleep. Because the wind was sharp, however, and whistled through the loft, Marco and Polo were soon joined on the army cot by Boots and Elvis, then Carlotta. Snuggled together, the five of them began to feel warm, and finally even Texas Jake gave up his throne on the rocking chair and came over, giving a quick nip to any cat who didn't move quite fast enough. Soon he was fur to fur with the other members of the Club of Mysteries.

They slept all through the night, rousing themselves only long enough to go to the Fishmonger for breakfast, then hurrying back to the warmth of the cot to sleep away most of the day and wait for evening.

Finally, when Polo opened his eyes once again, he realized that it was Friday, Boots's big day. He looked around and saw that Boots had already roused himself and was gliding softly across the floor and down the stairs to the garage below. The other cats waited patiently as it grew darker and darker outside, and a thin white slice of moon appeared through the window of the loft.

12
THE THIEVERY

An hour went by, perhaps two, and Marco wondered why he and Polo and Elvis and Carlotta should have to sit around the loft with their stomachs hungry just because Texas Jake had yet to eat.

What if Boots didn't pull it off, and there was no steak coming? Then they would all head to the Fishmonger anyway, but by that time all the good leftovers would be gone. The Persian, the Siamese, the Abyssinian, and all their buddies would have gotten there first.

But when he began, "Perhaps the rest of us could . . ." Texas Jake looked at him with such scorn that he closed his eyes and pretended it was only a vagrant thought.

Suddenly there was a rapid thud of pawsteps on the stairs, and Boots landed on the floor of the loft with a porterhouse steak in his jaws.

The aroma was incredible. It reminded Marco and Polo

of Christmas at the Neals', when a big rib roast would be cooking slowly in the oven. Of course, at the Neals', the roast was six feet away from them in the oven. Here, the meat was barely six inches from their noses.

All the cats crowded around to take a sniff. Marco could see the thick fat curling around the edge, the pink juices still dripping from the meat, the seared side where the meat had been browned, and if he had not feared for his life, he would have snatched the delicious steak away and eaten it himself.

Carefully Boots laid the steak in front of Texas Jake, who was climbing down off the army cot as fast as his lame legs would allow him. "A whole porterhouse steak, just out from under the broiler, and all for you," said Boots.

The fur had already risen on the back of the big cat's neck, and his tail had thickened, just in case any of the other cats had the mistaken idea that they were going to share the lovely piece of meat that smelled so delicious and was, in fact, still hot.

"Boots, you have proven yourself a cat of valor and distinction," Texas told him, crouching down over the porterhouse. He licked the steak all over and then, holding it firmly with his claws, began taking sharp bites along one edge, jerking his head with each bite.

"*Now* maybe the rest of us can go to the Fishmonger," Polo whispered, but Texas heard and gave a low growl. Not only did he want company while he ate, but he wanted the other cats to watch him enjoying himself.

"How did you *do* it, Boots?" Carlotta asked admiringly.

"Well, it wasn't easy," Boots said, licking one paw. "Not

easy at all. I thought to myself, Now which will upset Master more: if I take *his* steak or his friend's? I had seen him put them on the broiler pan, a large one for himself and a smaller one for his lady. If I stole the smaller one, I decided, he could divide the larger one in two and each of them could have a piece, while if I stole the larger one, Master would go hungry."

"Good thinking!" Elvis told him.

"But how did you get the meat outdoors? How did you get it here?" asked Polo.

"That was the lucky part." Boots thumped his tail against the floor as he recounted his adventure. "I had assumed that after I took the meat off the table, my master would chase me around the house for awhile, and I would hide under the bed where he couldn't reach me. Then, when the steak was cold and the meal was over, he would disgustedly toss me out the door along with the meat itself."

"So what happened?" the other cats asked eagerly.

"Well, as luck would have it, my master is not the world's best cook. In fact, when his lady friend comes to visit, he gets quite absentminded. He cooked the steak beautifully, but after he took it from the oven and put it on a platter, he neither removed the broiling pan from the oven nor did he turn the oven off. The pan grew hotter and hotter, and Master had to open the back door to let out the smoke. Then, after he seated his lady at the table, set the steak before her, and lit the candles, I pounced."

"You jumped right up on the table?" asked Carlotta.

"Well, I wasn't quite sure I could make it from floor to table, so I jumped on her lap first, *then* the table," Boots.

answered. "I had to watch out for those candles, too—I actually singed my tail—but I clamped my teeth over that juicy steak on her plate, ran to the edge of the table—right over the teacups and applesauce—and went flying through the open door."

The cats listened in rapt attention. "W-what did she *say?*" asked Carlotta.

"Not a word," said Boots. "She put one hand to her throat . . . I remember that. Maybe she uttered a little shriek. Yes, I'm sure now. She shrieked bloody murder, come to think of it. It wasn't until I was flying through the door that I heard my master bellow."

"He risked his home for you, Texas," Carlotta meowed, turning to the big yellow cat who was gobbling down his dinner, swallowing big hunks of the succulent meat so that he had to extend his neck and help each bite along. "He risked a warm bed and his meal ticket for years to come."

Texas licked his chops. "And don't think I'm not grateful, my lad," he purred. "Don't think I don't appreciate all that you've done."

At that very moment there was a human voice in the alley. "Oh, Boo-oots! Here, kitty, kitty, kitty! Nice kitty! Come on, Boots! Come on, pussycat, Daddy's little darling! Come on, sweetheart!"

"Uh-oh," said Boots. "I've never heard Master talk like that before."

"Well, don't answer till I've finished the steak," said Texas. "This is the best piece of meat I've ever had in my life, and I want to enjoy it right down to the bone."

"Here, kitty, kitty, kitty!" the voice continued calling. "Come on, Boots! Where are you?"

"They can't have eaten already," Boots mused. "I only left there ten minutes ago. They could hardly have finished their salads, much less the dessert course."

"Maybe he wants to tell you that all is forgiven," said Carlotta.

The cats waited silently while Texas Jake licked the bone and finally turned it over to Carlotta, in case there were any meaty tidbits he had overlooked.

By now the footsteps and the master's voice were almost outside the loft itself.

"Come on, you blasted cat! Where are you? When I find you, my little sweetheart, I'm going to wring your neck. Ruin *my* party, will you? Drive away *my* girl? Boots, you ever show your face around here and you are dog feed, I swear it!"

"You still think he loves me?" Boots said to Carlotta. He sighed wistfully. "I had it all—every comfort a cat could want—and now I've lost it."

But as the footsteps and the master's voice grew fainter and fainter, Texas Jake didn't seem to give a thought as to what would happen to Boots.

"Well, Boots," he said. "You have served me well. You too, Elvis. Now all I need is comfrey to heal my wounds, and you will all have proved you are capable of taking my place, should I no longer be able to serve."

He looked hard and long at Marco and Polo. "And so, lads, it's up to you."

13
THE MYSTERY OF SUN

All right, thought Marco. We'll go. But he wasn't going anywhere on an empty stomach.

Carlotta was still nibbling daintily on the bone Texas gave her, while Texas himself lay belly up, paws in the air, his head resting on Carlotta's back. But when the other cats were sure that Boots's master had gone, they went to the Fishmonger for dinner, and Boots, of course, had to tell his story of heroism to the Persian, the Abyssinian, and the Siamese all over again.

"What will you do if your master won't take you back?" the Persian purred, over a trout fillet.

"I'm sure one of you lads would take me in," Boots said.

No sooner were the words out of his mouth, however, than every cat there at the trash cans seemed to be looking the other way.

"Don't count on me," said the Siamese. "My mistress says I eat her out of house and home."

"Nor me," said the Persian. "My mistress says if she'd known how much I shed, she never would have bought me at all."

The Abyssinian turned to Boots. "My master says that one cat is one too many."

"Elvis?" asked Boots pleadingly.

"Not a chance," Elvis told him. "My master can hardly afford me."

"Marco and Polo?" Boots begged.

"It just isn't possible. With Jumper and Spinner about, the Neals have four cats as it is."

"Then you know what it means, lads. It's the animal shelter for me," Boots said mournfully.

A shudder went through the group, and for a moment the cats all stopped chewing.

"Why do they call it a shelter, do you suppose, when it's really death row?" mused the Siamese. "I've heard that they hold you there for ten days only, and if at the end of ten days no one adopts you, you're zapped."

Polo stared. He had never known this before. "Does that mean," he whispered to his brother, "that if the Neals had never come for us, we, too, would have been zapped?"

Marco, despite all his learning, had no answer.

"I have been to the shelter twice," the Abyssinian confessed. "Twice I have been adopted."

The other cats listened intently.

"If it ever happens to you, remember this," he said. "People like cats who behave most like themselves. It's a fact. Whenever anybody comes into the shelter you have to impress them with how human you are. When you meow, meow as expressively as possible, so that it sounds most like talking. When you sleep, lie with one paw over your eyes, as though shielding them from the light. Wipe your ears with your paws, rub your catnip all over your head. Act as though you have hands, not paws, and—this is most important of all—whenever possible, walk on your hind feet, if only for a second or two. That drives them absolutely nuts. They can't resist."

When dinner was over, Elvis climbed up on the wall and sang a few numbers with the Abyssinian, the Persian, and the Siamese. Polo especially enjoyed the hunting song:

> Oh, a-hunting we will go!
> A-hunting we will go,
> We'll catch a little mouse
> And drag him in the house,
> And never let him go!

After that, the members of the Club of Mysteries made their way back to Murphy's garage and, when they got there, discovered that Texas Jake was ready to hold an official meeting. Now that his belly was full, his mind was active.

"I have a mystery to discuss, my lads. How does the sun get from west to east again? Every morning it rises in the East, it travels across the sky, and sets in the West. In the morning, there it is, same as always, in the East. How?"

All the cats pondered this new mystery as they groomed themselves, licking their paws.

Polo opened his mouth first. "It goes back west through an underground tunnel," he said.

All the cats turned and stared at him.

Polo felt somewhat uneasy. "There *are* underground tunnels, you know," he said hastily. "There are pipes and tunnels for the sewers, so there *must* be one for the sun."

"In all the years I have been leader of the Club of Mysteries, I have never heard a more stupid answer," said Texas. "If the sun went through an underground tunnel at night, the earth beneath our paws at night would be hot. Quite the opposite, the earth beneath our paws is *cool*, stupid, *especially* at night. Your answer is a disgrace."

Polo was so embarrassed that he did the only thing he could think of, something even more stupid than his answer: He began to chase his tail.

Marco stopped him finally. "Settle down," he whispered. "*Really*, Polo, you are making a spectacle of yourself."

Polo hopped back up on the old army cot, but he was ashamed to look at Carlotta.

"I think I have the answer!" said Elvis. "The sun drops off the edge of the earth in the West, and comes back east in the river."

"That is almost as stupid as Polo's answer," said Texas. "I had expected better of you. The sun is fire, and if fire went into the river, the water would put it out. Where are the thinkers? Where is intellect and reason, my lads? Carlotta, what do you think?"

Carlotta looked shyly around the circle. "I think that the sun explodes at the end of every day and becomes the moon and stars. As to how it starts up again in the morning, I haven't the faintest idea."

It was such a beautiful thought, a poetic thought, that everyone forgave her, including Texas Jake.

"What about this?" said Boots. "It simply goes to sleep at the end of the day, and the birds wake it up in the morning. It streaks back through the sky at such speed that we don't even see it and there it is, in the East again."

"Imbeciles!" shouted Texas. "Morons! Each and every one of you!"

"I haven't spoken yet," came a voice, and Marco stood up.

Texas Jake peered over the edge of the rocker and his eyes became narrow slits.

"All the other idiots have spoken. What do *you* have to suggest?" he said.

Marco had been thinking about everything he had read in the newspaper at the bottom of his litter box back at the Neals. He remembered an article about the sun and the planets, the comets and the stars.

"I think that the earth is round and that it spins around. When the side we are on is facing the sun, it is day. When the side we are on is away from the sun, it is night. The sun doesn't move, *we* do."

At this, all the cats began to laugh so loudly that Murphy's loft was filled with their noise. The rocking chair moved back and forth, the army cot shook, and Elvis fell off the edge and onto the floor, he was laughing so hard.

"He thinks the earth is *round!*" howled Boots.

"He thinks the earth is *moving!*" gasped Elvis.

Texas Jake wiped his eyes with one paw. "Polo, I take it back. You are not the stupidest cat here, it's your brother. If the earth was round, we would all slide off. If the earth was moving, it would bump into things."

"Then . . . then how *does* the sun get from west back to the East again?" Marco asked.

Texas Jake drew himself up proudly there on the rocker. "Strange as it may seem," he said, "it is not the same sun! *You* may think you are looking at the same old sun—spring, summer, fall, and winter—but I tell you, lads, it is not. Just as a bird is born, and a flower unfolds, and a chicken hatches out of an egg, every morning we get a new sun, and every evening the light goes out."

"But where do the suns come from, a new one every morning?" asked Polo.

"It is born in the sky, in the wee hours of morning, so far out in space we cannot even see it until the first faint streaks of dawn paint the sky," Texas answered.

Carlotta snuggled down against him, gazing adoringly up into his face.

"And so, Marco—the cat who can *reeead*—let us have no more talk of round spinning earths. A more ridiculous idea I never heard," said Texas.

Marco walked over to the small window in the loft and looked out into the darkness. "But it *is* round," he said under his breath, "and it *does* spin."

It was hard, though, to think of going out on their journey—their dangerous journey to the dump—a fallen hero already, a clown, a joke. He had rather imagined Carlotta kissing him good-bye, and now, even though he might never see her again, she would always think that he was wrong and Texas Jake was right.

14
DOWN AT THE DUMP

Carlotta and Texas Jake were sound asleep, the other cats were sprawled here and there in the loft, and the two tabby brothers were bedded down on the pile of old newspapers.

"I wish we had never opened our mouths," said Polo. "They think we're idiots."

"We'll show them yet," Marco told him. "Now here's the plan. At the very crack of dawn, when it is just light enough to see what we're doing, we will sneak over to the dump and hope we can find the comfrey before Steak Knife and his gang wake up."

Polo snuggled up against him and promptly went to sleep, not because he was tired, but because he did not want to dwell on what lay ahead.

The first finger of daylight fell on Polo's face and seemed to stroke his whiskers. He scrunched up his eyes even tighter, wishing it away, but a bird beyond the window, who didn't know that winter was coming, launched into song.

Maybe Marco would forget about getting the comfrey, Polo thought. Maybe Marco would be extra hungry and decide to go back to the Neals'. Maybe it was raining outside. *Snowing,* even! A blizzard, and all the comfrey plants would be frozen. Maybe . . .

"It's time," came Marco's voice in his ear.

Polo gave a little sigh, rose up on his haunches, and followed his brother down the stairs.

The alley was quiet in the early morning. The only sounds were the *drip, drip* of water off the end of a drain-pipe and the faraway roar of a truck on the highway. Soft as snow, the tabby brothers started down the alley in the direction of the dump.

Polo, of course, wanted to stop for breakfast at the Fishmonger, but Marco forbade it.

"We need to be as light on our feet as possible, should we have to run for our lives," he said.

Since he never expected to run as fast as Steak Knife and the Over-the-Hill Gang anyway, and would probably lose his life one way or another, Polo preferred to die on a full stomach, but he was still too sleepy and cold to argue.

There was almost no traffic at the corner, so they crossed at once and started up the alley on the other side. On and on until the alley became an overgrown path, the path became a field, and the field, at long last, became the woods, which grew right up the hill.

Softly, softly they moved through the woods. All Polo

could hear was the sound of his own heart beating, beating, thumping out his terror.

Who knew where the Over-the-Hill Gang was hiding, under what bank they were sleeping, behind which rock, inside which log? All it would take was one bleary eye opening in the breeze, one quizzical face peering out from behind a tree, one scruffy ear catching a single noise—the snap of a twig, the crackle of a leaf, a pebble, perhaps, skidding along the path.

But Marco and Polo were steadfast, and moved like moonlight, making no sound.

The woods were even darker than Polo imagined they could be in the early morning. If the Over-the-Hill Gang had not caught them in the field, they would surely catch them here. There were all those holes in the stumps of trees, all those hollows in logs, all the ditches in dirt, the nests in leaves, the caves in rocks, plus the many branches above, where a band of rowdy cats might stay the night. They could be looking down on Marco and Polo this very minute, plotting their next move.

Yet somehow, nothing happened. Scarcely breathing, the tabbies made their way through the woods and up the hill. At the top, they found themselves looking down on a broad expanse of dump.

This was the real test, for here Steak Knife and his Over-the-Hill Gang could be almost anywhere—inside old rusty oil drums, beneath a mound of tires, in boxes, broken-down refrigerators, old cars, old boots. . . .

Marco and Polo started down into the dump and then they stopped in terror. For there on a fence was a collection

of tails. Rat tails, cat tails, mouse tails, raccoon tails, bird tails, squirrel tails, and even the tail of a small dog. They were draped over the fence like trophies, and there must have been a dozen.

"Don't look," said Marco. "Just keep going, and don't make a sound." They set off again single file, trying not to think about what they had seen, weaving this way and that among the trash.

At one point Polo saw a paw sticking out of a milk can, and a tail hanging over the edge of a box.

But nothing moved, nothing stirred, nothing grunted. They went on, checking every weed, every stem, every stalk, and had just hopped over an old stove pipe when they saw, straight ahead, some comfrey, just as Carlotta had described it, the leaves growing first one way, then another. They could see that it was different from foxglove, and how easily they had mistaken one for the other.

Marco and Polo could scarcely believe their good fortune. By some miracle they had made it through the dump and found their prize at last.

Carefully each cat pulled up a stalk with his teeth, then looked back up the hill toward the long return journey. They gave each other a mournful look, a meaningful look—a sort of "we-who-are-about-to-die" look. And then they started home.

The climb back up the hill from the dump did not seem much different from when they climbed up through the woods on the other side, but once they reached the top and headed down into the trees, things seemed more alive.

Polo carefully studied the landscape below. He did not see any person, any dog, any cat . . . not even a rat or a mouse. But every so often something seemed to move, stir, flick, swish, crawl, scurry, dash, creep. A paw, perhaps—a tail, a whisker. He couldn't really say he had seen anything for sure, and yet . . . ?

Stealthily, stealthily they went on, weaving in and out of trees. They were almost halfway through the woods when a sort of murmuring began. At first Polo thought he only imagined it, but then the murmurs became words and the words a drumbeat:

> Com-frey,
> Com-frey,
> They've got
> Our com-frey.
> Slice 'em up,
> Dice 'em up,
> Rough 'em up,
> Tough 'em up,
> Get the
> Com-frey,
> Com-frey,
> Com-frey. . . .

Polo looked behind him only once, and that was enough. The mangy, scraggly, rat-tailed hooligan of a cat was far behind him on the path, and following Steak Knife was his dirty, scruffy, noisy bunch of felines.

15
MISSION ACCOMPLISHED . . . ALMOST

The Over-the-Hill Gang was howling now. The tabby brothers didn't think they had ever heard such terrible sounds except, perhaps, from their own throats when the Neals took them to the vet. Marco turned once to see the gang's awful mouths wide open, their tails thick as baseball bats, their ears flat, their eyes flashing.

It was difficult to meow with the comfrey between his teeth, he discovered.

It was hard to keep running when he was overweight.

It wasn't easy to think, when any moment the Over-the-Hill Gang could catch up with them and tear them ear to tail.

But a strange thing happened on their flight down the alley. Instead of the howls gaining on them, the sounds began to die away. Instead of the thud of padded feet growing louder, the noises grew fainter and fainter until, at last, when Marco and Polo reached the corner by the Fishmonger and raced across the street, barely escaping the wheels of a passing truck, there was only the faintest sound behind them. And they didn't look back again until they were inside the door of Murphy's garage.

They skidded to a stop, sides heaving. Whatever was out there didn't follow them in. Could this be? Would Steak Knife and his gang really allow them to get away with stealing their comfrey to make a rival cat strong again? Had the race been too much for that scruffy crew? It hardly seemed possible. But Marco and Polo were too tired to worry about it further, and hastily tore up the stairs to the loft above.

Texas Jake was asleep in the rocking chair. When he heard their paws on the floor, however, he opened one eye. And when he saw the comfrey between their teeth, the big yellow cat with the white belly sat up and frankly stared.

Carlotta gave a little gasp and nudged Boots and Elvis, who were asleep on the army cot.

"They did it, Texas!" she purred admiringly. "They brought you the comfrey."

Texas Jake leaned so far over the edge of the rocker it looked as though he would surely fall.

"It *looks* like comfrey," he agreed. "*Smells* like comfrey." Then he hopped right down and looked at the sprigs up close. "Good job, lads!" he said at last. "It *is* comfrey! Comfrey, indeed!"

"And I hope," Marco panted, "that you will consider this my apology for attacking you."

"I shall forget it ever happened," said Texas, but Marco wasn't entirely convinced.

He and Polo were so exhausted that all they could do was lie on their sides and pant. Carlotta, of course, set right to work licking the leaves of the comfrey to make them sticky and wet. Then Texas Jake lay down on them and rolled about, rubbing his wounded leg and side over the sticky wet leaves until some of them actually stuck to his stitches. He was fairly plastered in comfrey.

And when Marco and Polo caught their breath and explained all they had gone through to get the comfrey leaves that would heal their lame leader, the other cats could not help but be impressed.

"Aren't they wonderful, Texas?" Carlotta purred. "Aren't they splendid?"

But Texas Jake suddenly rose to his feet, the comfrey still sticking to one leg. "Do you know what you have done?" he thundered, looking straight at the tabbies.

Marco and Polo stared at him. What they had done? They had brought him comfrey, of course! They had done what they said they would do. But there was something about the tone of Texas Jake's voice that made them cautious.

"You may *think* the Over-the-Hill Gang stopped following you far back in the field, but I assure you that Steak Knife did not. And even if he didn't come as far as Murphy's garage, he undoubtedly watched you run down the alley and knows just where you turned in. You have given away the meeting place of the Club of Mysteries, you fools!"

"Steak Knife didn't know it before?" Marco asked.

"If he knew before, his gang would have been over here."

"W-what will happen now?" asked Polo, beginning to shake.

"Anything could happen," said Texas, pacing the loft, and Marco was surprised to discover that he was no longer limping at all. Either the comfrey had healed his leg in a matter of minutes or he was stronger than he had appeared.

A hush fell over the loft. Elvis and Boots, who had been envious of Marco and Polo's accomplishment only moments before, now looked at them with scorn.

"And you thought *you* could be our leader?" Boots chided.

Carlotta was frightened indeed. "Texas, what will we do?" she meowed.

"We will wait," Texas told her. "And if the Over-the-Hill Gang comes calling, Marco and Polo here, who led the gang to our club house, will just have to lead them back out again."

Texas Jake wasn't Commander in Chief, Lord of the Loft, King of the Alley, and Cat Supreme for nothing, and he told them his plan.

The cats did not leave the loft all morning. The October wind made the loft colder still. Leaves which had died on the trees and had not yet come down scratched like fingernails against the sides of Murphy's garage. The window at the back, which had no glass at all, had a thin coat of frost on the sill, and the air held a heavy damp smell that spoke of snow.

As morning turned into afternoon, and afternoon into evening, the cats started at every sound. There had been the familiar sound of Mr. Murphy getting into his car below, then returning. The sound of the garbage truck coming down the alley, the rattling of trash cans, the traffic out on the street by the Fishmonger, and children coming to and from school.

But there were other sounds, too—odd sounds, small sounds, little creaks and thuds and squeaks that none of the cats had noticed before. Once Marco peered down into the alley and was sure he saw Steak Knife slouching around a corner, his nose sniffing this way and that.

Marco fell asleep at last, a troubled sleep. He awoke more than once to find his jaws trembling and his paws jerking in response to some dream, but he settled down again on the old army cot beside the others as the wind blew harder, bringing with it the first snowflakes of the season.

Suddenly Marco heard a noise right by his ear. Something nibbled it, in fact, and when he gave it a twitch, Timothy Mouse, Esquire, landed right between his paws.

Marco's first thought was that he would not have to go out for dinner, that dinner had come to him. But this was dinner that wouldn't shut up.

"Marco! Listen to me!" Timothy squeaked, hardly able to breathe because the cat held him so securely in his paws. "The Over-the-Hill Gang is coming this way. I just saw them all crossing the street by the Fishmonger."

16
SAVING THEIR SKINS

Instantly Marco was awake, the other cats also. As Timothy squeaked out his story again, this time from one of the rafters above, where Texas wouldn't be tempted to taste him, the cats rose to their feet as the first sound of pawsteps sounded on the stairs below.

But they all knew what to do. Before the first member of the Over-the-Hill Gang reached the loft, Carlotta jumped onto Texas's back as he had told her, and Texas, in turn, leaped up on a hat rack in a far dark corner of the loft, to hide her and protect her with his life if necessary.

When Steak Knife and his rowdy, scraggly, mangy band of cats reached the top step, however, the other members of the Club of Mysteries streaked toward the open window at the back and, one by one, quick as lightning, landed on the shed below. Howling like the wind, the Over-the-Hill Gang followed.

With Marco in the lead, running faster than he had ever run in his life, then Polo, making terrified little bleats, followed by Boots and Elvis, they charged down the alley, around a corner, up on a fence, over the limb of a leaning tree, along the fence on the other side, and across a shed to the yard beyond.

Only Marco could read the sign on the fence: BEWARE OF THE DOG.

The fence rattled as the cats ran along the top—Marco, Polo, Boots, and Elvis, then Steak Knife and all the other scruffy-haired, dirty-nosed, rag-tag ruffians of the Over-the-Hill Gang.

His heart beating fiercely, Marco leaped down onto the roof of Bertram's doghouse with a thud, and started across the yard, the other cats not far behind, Steak Knife's scraggly claws making a scratchy sound as they hit the roof of the doghouse.

There was a sudden roar, and the ground shook as the huge mastiff shot out of his doghouse like a cannonball.

Cats scattered across the yard like fireworks. Marco, Polo, Boots, and Elvis knew what to expect, of course, and were ready to make their escape. But the Over-the-Hill Gang had only been intent on catching the members of the Club of Mysteries, and did not know which way to run. Cats here, cats there—skittering, scattering, scratching, screeching—tails and paws in huge confusion.

It was like an army gone berserk. It was every cat for himself. Such howling and yowling and braying Marco and Polo had never heard, and a moment later the two tabby brothers, along with Boots and Elvis, were up on the fence

again, down the other side, and heading back up the alley toward Murphy's loft.

Into the open door of the garage.

Under Murphy's car to the other side.

Up the dusty stairs to the loft above, where Texas Jake and Carlotta were waiting for them.

"Well done, my lads! Well done, indeed!" cried Texas. "Steak Knife and his gang will not be coming back anytime soon, I'll wager."

And with much panting and laughter, Marco, Polo, Boots, and Elvis described the look of surprise on Steak Knife's scruffy face when Bertram came roaring out of his doghouse.

Texas Jake climbed up on his rocker again and looked down on the others assembled below.

"Well, lads, when—and if—these old bones of mine retire as leader of the Club of Mysteries, one of you will be taking my place. Who shall it be? A cat who can compose a song? A cat who can lick her master's wounds? A feline who can steal a steak? Or a cat—or cats—who can brave the hooligans at the dump and bring home the comfrey? Should we vote?"

And then, before anyone could answer, Texas answered for them: "Of course not! If we took a vote, each cat would, of course, vote for himself. So let's hear no more talk of Texas Jake retiring."

"Now just a minute, Texas," said Carlotta. "I am withdrawing my name from nomination for personal reasons. And if I am not going to be in the running, then I think I have every right to vote."

All the cats turned and looked at the she-cat. It seemed only fair, but not one of them was sure she would vote for him, for Carlotta was a friend of many but the true love of none.

"All right," said Texas, after a pause. "As long as we are talking *some* day, far away, off in the future, a no-one-knows-when day."

All the members of the Club of Mysteries waited. What would her answer be?

But Carlotta wasn't Carlotta for nothing. She thought about it a long time, and at last she purred, "There is nothing as beautiful as a song . . ."

Elvis's chest swelled, and he looked around confidently.

"Or as clever as stealing a steak off a master's plate . . ."

Boots grinned.

"Or as brave as facing the Over-the-Hill Gang at the dump. . . ."

Marco and Polo each felt hopeful.

"All of these things take intelligence and talent, bravery and cunning. But if you leave it to me, Texas, I can only speak the words that come from my heart. Therefore, my answer is . . ."

The cats held their breath.

"I would choose the cat among you who will be kindest to my kittens."

"Kittens?" gasped Marco and Polo.

"Kittens?" cried Texas Jake. "When are you expecting kittens?"

"When there's snow on the ground and the wind blows

cold and the alley is covered with ice. Then I will have my kittens," Carlotta said.

Texas drew himself up to his fullest height, his yellow chest thrust out above his white belly, and said in his deepest, most powerful voice, "Then I, my dear Carlotta, being the strongest cat here, shall teach your kittens to defend their mother against any harm that could befall her."

"But I," said Elvis, prancing back and forth before the calico cat as though he were onstage, "shall teach them to enjoy the art of singing. I shall make trios, or quartets, or quintets of your kittens."

"I, being the most clever, shall teach them to hunt," said Boots.

"I will teach them to read," Marco promised.

The calico cat turned her gentle eyes on Polo. "Have you anything to offer my kittens?" she asked.

"Well," said Polo, "if they are to learn to fight, to sing, to hunt, and to read, then I guess I'll have to teach them to enjoy themselves, the art of letting go." He whirled around a time or two in pursuit of his tail to demonstrate.

Carlotta simply smiled. She stood up and stretched and then, touching each cat briefly on the nose, said, "Now I must go. I have a secret place where I can be alone, so don't try to find me. When you see me next, I shall be the mother of kittens."

The he-cats followed her down the steps of the loft and watched her trot daintily down the alley, tail in the air. She *did* look a bit hefty, Marco thought—a bit wide at the sides. In fact, she was positively round, now that she'd mentioned it. He had thought she simply had been enjoying herself a little more than usual at the Fishmonger.

Marco looked at Boots. "Do you think your master will take you back?"

"Oh, I'm sure of it," said Boots. "Now that his lady friend has left him, he'll need a cat to curl up in his lap more than ever—even a cat who steals his dinner."

"Well, good luck to you then," said Polo.

"Good-bye," said Elvis to Texas Jake as he left for the Fishmonger. "Take care of your leg."

"Till it snows, then, and ice covers the alley," said the big yellow cat. "Then we shall have our next meeting."

As the two tabbies went down the alley toward the Neals' backyard, the wind felt sharp, and ruffled their fur. They were glad when at last they pushed through the gate and reached the back porch, where they meowed loudly.

"What have *you* two been up to?" Mrs. Neal said, opening the door. "You look like something that came from the dump. In fact, you *smell* like a dump. Where in the world do you cats go when I let you out, that's what I'd like to know."

Polo would have been happy to tell her, but humans, for all their smarts, had never bothered to learn cat language.

Nevertheless, there was food in their porcelain dish, water in their bowl, and as soon as Jumper and Spinner heard Marco and Polo coming, they leaped out of the velveteen basket and let the older cats have their bed. There were always stories to be told when Marco and Polo went off on an adventure and, as Marco said, a story is best told from a prone position.

"Tell us! Tell us!" Spinner said, whirling around the room in anticipation.

"What did you do this time? Where did you go? What did you see?" asked Jumper, leaping from chair to chair.

"Lie down and be quiet and we shall tell you," Marco said, and, as always, the story that was told was not quite the way it had happened.

"To get to the comfrey that would heal Texas Jake," Marco began, "we had to climb a mountain."

"A *high* mountain," added Polo. "With snow!"

"We had to fight an army of ruffians and scalawags," said Marco.

"With claws like daggers!" added Polo.

"And even after we got the comfrey and brought it back, we had to face a beast," said Marco.

"A monster," said Polo. "A huge and terrible monster with a roar that could wake a village."

"Start at the beginning," said Spinner, and the story began.

What's next for Marco and Polo?
Here's a preview of *Carlotta's Kittens.*

One
Asking Around

When the air was cold, and the sky was gray, and the wind blew its frosty breath through every crack and crevice, Marco and Polo thought of Carlotta. The thick white snow beyond the window sparkled in the noonday sun. At night it glistened in the soft yellow light of the streetlamps. It silently snuggled up against doors and garden walls. And somewhere, they didn't know where, the beautiful calico cat was having her kittens.

"I wonder if she's safe," said Marco, the larger of the tabbies.

"I wonder if she's warm," said Polo, his brother, who was known, now and then, to chase his tail.

And they both wondered whether she was getting enough to eat, or whether she was eating anything at all. Being male cats, they had no idea what it was like to be called "Carlotta" one day, and "Mother" the next.

And then Marco said what they were both thinking: "What if some other cat from the Club of Mysteries finds her first, and decides to be daddy to her kittens?"

All the cats in the Club of Mysteries wanted to be special in Carlotta's eyes. Each of them dreamed of someday doing something so brave, so noble, that the beautiful calico cat, who was a friend to all but the true love of none, would think him best. But none of them knew where she had gone to have her kittens, only that she was going. And now that autumn had changed to winter, and the world had turned to ice, the cats worried.

Marco crawled out of the velveteen basket and stretched himself, rump in the air. His belly was so round that it grazed the floor, and he opened his mouth and gave an enormous yawn.

"I think I'll trot over to the Club to see what's what," he said.

Polo tried to pretend he didn't hear. He tried to pretend he didn't see. When he dreamed of protecting Carlotta and her kittens, he rather imagined seeing them lined up outside the picture window, and that he would meow till his mistress let them in. He didn't think about actually going out after them. He didn't think *cold*. He didn't think *snow*. He didn't think *freeze your tail off and your whiskers too*.

Nonetheless, if Marco was going, Polo was going. He couldn't stand the thought of Marco finding the calico cat and snuggling up beside her, Polo not included. So he left the warmth of the velveteen basket too. When Jumper and Spinner, the kittens the Neals had adopted, saw them leaving, they asked, "When will *we* be old enough to join the Club of Mysteries?" for they had heard the tales of adventure the tabbies had told.

"Not for a long time yet," said Marco grandly. "A very long time." And with his tail in the air, he walked to the back door of the Neals' house, lifted his head, and yowled. Polo joined in.

"I hear you! I hear you!"Mrs. Neal said, coming in from the kitchen in her slippers. "I don't understand you two, I really don't. You wait until the coldest day of the year, and then you decide you want to go out prowling. Where you go and what you do is a mystery to me, because you have everything you could possibly want right inside these four walls."

Marco tried to tell her, but she never understood the language. He tried to explain it was the walls themselves they needed to escape from now and then, but the back door opened, and a moment later he and Polo stepped into three inches of snow. Polo started to back up, but with a nudge of her foot, Mrs. Neal propelled him off the step, and the door clicked behind him.

Marco lifted his right front paw and shook it, then his left front paw. He picked up his right hind foot and shook it, then his left. Polo tried to pick up three feet at one time and promptly fell on his nose.

"Why does it have to be so cold?" he asked, his teeth chattering. He always asked his brother these questions, because Marco could read. Somehow Marco had taught himself the alphabet while sitting in his litter box, studying the newspaper there at the bottom. Polo just did his business and climbed out.

"It is cold," said Marco, "because it is not hot. And the opposite of hot is cold."

"Oh," Polo said, and wished for the twentieth time that he were even half as smart as his brother.

They delicately crossed the yard, stepping in the footprints made by Mr. Neal that morning when he had gone out to his car. Then they jumped up on the fence, over the gate, and down into the alley.

The mouse named Timothy scurried under a garbage-can lid when he saw them coming. He had an understanding with the tabby brothers that they would never harm him. Still, Marco forgot sometimes, and pounced. He'd hold the little mouse tight in his paws for a moment or two before letting him go, and Timothy would prefer not to go through that ordeal again.

The snow was dazzling in the morning sun, but not so dazzling that Polo didn't see the mouse.

"Good morning, Timothy," he called. "Have you seen Carlotta lately?"

"The calico she-cat with the plump belly?" asked Timothy. "I heard she went off somewhere to have her kittens."

"But where?" asked Marco.

"Here . . . there . . . could be anywhere," Timothy answered. "Mostly I just stay out of her way. Any she-cat who has just had kittens is hungry, and I don't want to be on her menu." And the little mouse disappeared.

The next creature the tabby brothers encountered was the black crow that scavenged around the neighborhood.

"Good morning," called Marco. "Have you, by chance, seen Carlotta and her kittens?"

"Ah!" The crow stopped picking at a dead squirrel on the pavement and fixed his eye on Marco. Marco and Polo were trying not to look at the squirrel. "She's had her kittens, has she? Well, if she doesn't take care, one will get run over by a car, one will die of cold, one will die of hunger, one will get attacked by a vicious dog, and I shall have my choice of dishes for a week."

"How can you say such things?" cried Polo. "Doesn't it ruin your appetite?"

"Not at all, not at all," said the crow. "We are the street cleaners—pickers, if you will—of society. One day a possum is dead upon the highway, and the next it's gone. And who has come by to clean up the mess? Your friendly, efficient neighborhood crow, that's who."

"But you *haven't* seen them, have you? You haven't breakfasted on fillet of kitten, I hope?" Marco asked.

"No, but if you see Carlotta, tell her to keep her kittens close to her at all times, especially when crossing the street. A flat cat is of no use whatsoever to its mother, but it *does* make a tasty pancake."

At this the tabbies were more determined than ever to find their calico friend, and finally they reached Murphy's garage, where the Club of Mysteries held its meetings. It wasn't too long ago that Marco and Polo had become members, having successfully solved one of life's great mysteries that Texas Jake, the leader, had assigned them—namely, where does water go when it rains? They had never felt that the big yellow cat approved of them 100 percent. But Murphy's garage was as good a place as any to get out of the wind, catch up on neighborhood gossip, and—most important—see Carlotta. And so they crept inside and up the dusty stairs to the loft above. There they discovered a meeting already in progress; no one had waited for them.

On an old rocking chair in the center of the floor sat the big yellow cat, the scars from many battles on his skin. Texas Jake inched himself forward until both his nose and his claws were overhanging the seat of the chair, and glowered at Marco and Polo with his huge yellow eyes.

"Well, well, lads, look what we have here! Our two newest members. We thought for sure we had frightened you off," he said.

"Never," said Marco, prepared to take his place with the best of them. "We wondered if anyone has seen Carlotta, and whether or not she has had her kittens."

"We're all wondering the same thing," said Boots, the smallest of the cats, with brown on the ends of his four white paws. "The last any of us has seen of her was the day she announced she was going away for a while and did not want to be disturbed."

"I have even been by her master's home, and heard him calling her, but she didn't come," said Elvis, a coal-black cat with green eyes.

"Then here's what we shall do," said Texas Jake, Commander in Chief, King of the Alley, Lord of the Loft, the Cat Supreme. "Everyone knows that new kittens are in danger until they're old enough to take care of themselves, and it's up to us to protect Carlotta and her litter.

Boots, you look for her tracks in the snow; Elvis, you watch for her at the Fishmonger; and *you*," he said, turning to the tabbies, "must stand guard outside the door to Murphy's garage—sentinels, if you will. Keep your eyes on the alley and your ears to the wind, and report back to me twice a day."

"And you, Texas Jake. What will *you* do?" asked Marco boldly.

The big cat rolled his eyes one way, then rolled them the other. "I'll wait until you bring Carlotta and her kittens to me," he said. "*Then,* my lads, we will decide what is what."